in association with

The New York Public Library

presents

a faithful facsimile of
the prompt copy of

David Copperfield

belonging to the author,

Charles Dickens

Together with the emended script,
suitable for public performance

The author's
personal prompt copy

David Copperfield

The author's personal prompt copy

David Copperfield

as scripted and performed by

Charles Dickens

LEVENGER PRESS

Published by Levenger Press
420 South Congress Avenue
Delray Beach, Florida 33445 USA
Levengerpress.com 800.544.0880

First Edition 2014

Portrait of Charles Dickens (1858). Engraved by Daniel John Pound after the daguerreotype portrait by John Jabez Edwin Mayall. The New York Public Library, Henry W. and Albert A. Berg Collection of English and American Literature. Image ID: 483482.

The original prompt copy from which this facsimile has been produced is owned by The New York Public Library and resides in the Henry W. and Albert A. Berg Collection of English and American Literature, The New York Public Library, Astor, Lenox and Tilden Foundations.

nypl.org

Library of Congress Cataloging-in-Publication Data

Dickens, Charles, 1812-1870.
David Copperfield : the author's personal prompt copy as scripted and performed by Charles Dickens. -- First edition.
pages cm
Includes bibliographical references.
ISBN 978-1-929154-54-8
1. Young men--Fiction. 2. Orphans--Fiction. 3. England--Social life and customs--19th century--Fiction. 4. Autobiographical fiction. 5. Bildungsromans. I. Title.
PR4558.A1 2014
823'.8--dc23

2014026144

Printed on acid-free paper from a renewable, sustainable source and containing 30% post-consumer recovered fiber, using soy-blended inks. Manufactured by Worzalla, an environmentally responsible printer.

Cover and book design by Danielle Furci
Image editing by Alfred Guerra
Mim Harrison, Editor

Printed in the USA

Contents

CHARLES DICKENS,

FROM A PHOTOGRAPH TAKEN AT THE TIME WHEN HE WAS WRITING "DAVID COPPERFIELD".

Introduction

CHARLES DICKENS'S fictional characters were known to his contemporaries as vividly alive companions, perhaps even more so than they are to us. Like us, the Victorians delighted in experiencing the jagged and smooth edges of these characters' personalities; hearing the idiosyncratic cadences and tone of their speech; watching them amble down a London street, or spoon porridge into their mouths; and, above all, witnessing the unspooling of their interior lives through the flickering light and shade of hope and fear, as they journey from disappointment to triumph, and from love to death. We are grateful to the creator of these characters for having shared with us everything that his benevolent, all-seeing eye has witnessed. But these characters would not live in our imaginations quite so vividly had not Dickens's richness of characterization and psychological insight been joined to the extraordinary voice that animates his books. An enchanting paradox of Dickens's novels is that regardless of the character who is speaking with such seeming naturalness, as if he or she were a real person independent of a literary creator, and whose actions we follow with such affectionate concern, sympathy, fear, or loathing, we cleave above all to the narrator's companionable, wise, occasionally ironic, and reassuring voice.

Great novelists who work their magic chiefly through character and story make us believe that we are reading an intimate letter—a friend's revelations about his circle of friends and acquaintances—rather than a fictional narrative. We are as taken by the teller (or the teller's fictional persona) as the tale, because it is the tone and manner of telling, the sensibility infusing the narrator's voice, that makes the characters real. The effect of this psychological alchemy was probably more intense for Dickens's contemporaries than for us, because most of Dickens's novels first appeared in serial form. The Dickens scholar Malcolm Andrews insightfully surmised that as Dickens's readers awaited the appearance of a novel's next installment, which would arrive by mail at their homes some weeks in the future, their recollections of what they had read and their anticipation of what might happen to their favorite characters had mingled in their minds with their recollections about, and hopes for, their own friends and family. In fact, as Andrews pointed out, this incorporation of Dickens's fictional world into his readers' daily lives was remarked upon in the Dickens obituary that appeared in *The Illustrated London News*, in which the writer observed that serial publication "aided the experience of this immediate personal companionship between the writer and reader. It was just as if we received a letter or a visit, at regular intervals, from a kindly observant gossip [...] The course of his narrative seemed to run on, somehow, almost simultaneously with the real progress of events, only keeping a little behind, so that he might have time to write down whatever happened, and to tell us."

His journey to the public stage as a performer of his own works was not quick or smooth.

But, of course, readers knew that they were reading fiction, not reportage. We therefore should not be surprised that Dickens's readers clamored to hear and see him perform his works, in order that they might witness how his creations came alive in their creator, as he stood before them on a stage. Fortunately, Dickens was a talented and experienced actor, which enabled him to satisfy his readers' desire. But his journey to the public stage as a performer of his own works was not quick or smooth.

Dickens had, since the late 1830s, given private readings of his works to small groups of friends and acquaintances (he also produced and acted in amateur theatricals). But his first public performance of any of his works did not occur until the evenings of December 27, 28, and 29, 1853, in Birmingham, each time before a sold-out house of two thousand. He performed gratis, for the benefit of the newly established Birmingham and Midland Institute, which was dedicated to adult education in the sciences and technology, and he read *A Christmas Carol* on the first and third evenings, between which he performed *The Cricket on the Hearth*, another of his Christmas tales. Though reviewers observed that he had omitted portions of the published text of *A Christmas Carol*, the performance still took over three hours, and Dickens realized that he

would have to shrink the text considerably, if he hoped to hold an audience's attention throughout its reading. (No doubt he was motivated also by the exhaustion brought on by so lengthy a performance.) From this necessity was born the first of his performance, or prompt, copies—*A Christmas Carol*—which is among the thirteen housed in the Berg Collection at The New York Public Library. (Levenger Press produced a handsome facsimile edition of this volume in 2009.) For the next several years, he read *A Christmas Carol* publicly, gratis, on fifteen occasions (chiefly in December, but also in spring and fall, and on three occasions, in June and July), for various charities, notably those that promoted literacy and child welfare.

But the idea of performing for his own profit had attracted him at least as early as 1846, when he broached the possibility in a letter to his friend and future biographer, John Forster. "A great deal of money might possibly be made," the formerly impoverished author surmised, though he worried that such an action might be *infra dig*—that is, beneath his dignity. Forster assured him that his concern was well founded, warning him that if he carried out his intention, he would damage his reputation as a gentleman, which for an upper-middle-class Victorian was a mortifying prospect. Both Dickens and Forster were, of course, aware of the pervasive middle-class view of actors and theatrical productions as morally unsavory, a bias that had taken root during the Evangelical reform movement of the century's early decades, and that was related to the moral, psychological, and political implications of dissembling, in a society whose middle class was devoted to propriety, and its ruling class to stability. Though prominent authors such as the Romantic poet Samuel Taylor Coleridge and the literary critic William Hazlitt had read in public to critical acclaim, they were lecturing—communicating ideas—not acting out emotions in the guise of different characters.

Forster assured him that if he carried out his intention, he would damage his reputation as a gentleman, which for an upper-middle-class Victorian was a mortifying prospect.

It is true that by mid-century, affordable "Penny Readings" of the works of popular, contemporary authors like Dickens, as well as great writers of the past, like Shakespeare, had become a common feature of urban English life (many of the event organizers allowing free admission to "Working Men & their Wives," as contemporary posters proclaimed). We learn from Andrews that between October 1857 and April 1858, the month in which Dickens became a professional reader, nine Staffordshire towns drew between sixty and seventy thousand customers to their Penny Readings, a phenomenon that seems to have been replicated across England. (Clearly, when Dickens took to the professional stage in April 1858, he had cast himself upon a cresting wave.) These programs reflected social reformers' attempt to encourage the masses to learn to read. But the performance readers at these events were not the authors of the works, nor did they read dramatically, which is to say, they did not attempt to impersonate the characters whose words they were reading. The evolution of Dickens's performances bears witness to this bias, as the readings of the first several years of his public, charity readings were less dramatic, in the sense of the performer adopting the persona of the character speaking, than those dating from his professional performing career.

Public performances of popular tales would bring him the love and adulation, in addition to the money, he craved.

Several motives intersected in the late 1850s to bring Dickens to the professional stage. As he explained to Forster, the expense of maintaining his newly bought country home, Gad's Hill Place, was high, and professional readings would help defray these costs. But two other motives also influenced his decision. First, his marriage was dissolving, and, as he admitted to Forster, he needed a distraction from that source of anxiety at a time when writing had become difficult. Second, the recently published *Little Dorritt*, though a commercial success, had been a critical disappointment, and this had shaken his confidence as a writer. Public performances of popular tales would bring him the love and adulation, in addition to the money, he craved. When Dickens again wrote to Forster, toward the end of March 1858, about the proposition to turn professional, having already performed for charities on eighteen occasions, he argued, "But do you quite consider that the public exhibition of oneself takes place equally, whosoever may get the money?" Clearly, both Dickens and Forster recognized that an author reading his stories and novels publicly, even for charity, would, in the minds of many, be tainted with vulgarity. Now,

Dickens was proposing to embark on a much more intense program of public readings for his own gain, calculated to earn him, as he had put it in 1846, "a great deal of money."

Despite Forster's objections, the public's enthusiastic reaction to Dickens's 1853 Birmingham performances and to the subsequent charitable readings eventually emboldened him to take to the stage professionally. This he did on April 29, 1858, in London's St. Martin's Hall, later called the Queen's Theatre. Unsurprisingly, he chose to read *A Christmas Carol*, which had served as the only reading at all but one of his eighteen charitable performances. He knew it to be a crowd favorite regardless of the season. But he must have been at least somewhat apprehensive about taking the "Plunge" (as he called his transformation into a professional performer), since his introduction to his performance included the defensive assurance, "I have satisfied myself that it [i.e., performing for money] can involve no possible compromise of the credit and independence of literature." Most reviewers were not persuaded; they accused him of cheapening himself and his art. But Dickens's public did not agree. His professional readings would prove as popular as the charitable ones, and by the time of his death, in 1870, he had given five hundred forty-eight public readings, all but twenty-eight for profit; *A Christmas Carol* had been read at a quarter of all of the performances.

Most reviewers accused him of cheapening himself and his art. But Dickens's public did not agree.

The literary scholar Philip Collins has documented the prodigious profits that Dickens earned from his professional readings. They averaged over £1000 for a month of performances (about forty), at a time when he earned less than £3000 annually from his publications. Of course, because of the great expenditure of energy demanded by so full a performance schedule, and because Dickens still very much wanted to write, he could not perform as often as that for more than a few months a year. Tickets at the great majority of his readings were priced at five shillings (for the "Farewell" reading tour of 1870, the price went up to seven shillings), though "some" seats, as

Dickens insisted, were always put aside at a cost of one shilling, because he wanted members of the working class in attendance. But we should be aware that an 1850s shilling would now equal about six dollars. Would we today expect the parent of what we call a "working poor" family, but lacking our social safety net of food stamps and medical care, to spend six dollars on a literary reading? (In his 1870 biography of Dickens, Shelton Mackenzie recalls discovering in a locksmith's shop a group of about twenty men and women who had organized themselves into a reading group in order to be able to afford the shilling cost of a monthly subscription to a Dickens serial, each of them contributing one penny.) Even more extravagant were the admission prices charged for Dickens's American tour for the winter of 1867-1868. Tickets to these performances sold for two dollars apiece, at a time when an American laborer earned one dollar a day. (Scalped tickets sold for twenty-six dollars.) At the tour's conclusion, Dickens had realized a net profit of over £19,000. (Had he not insisted on being paid in gold, fearing that America's post-Civil War currency was unstable, he would have netted £32,000.) To appreciate the immense purchasing power of £19,000 in that period, consider that in 1868, a solidly middle-class London annual income, which could maintain a household of from two to five servants, ranged from £300 to £1000. All this is not to deny Dickens's good intentions, but to acknowledge what he himself declared: he took the "Plunge" in order to make "a great deal of money."

Tickets to these performances sold for two dollars apiece, at a time when an American laborer earned one dollar a day.

The process whereby Dickens created the *David Copperfield* performance copy differed in one important respect from the way he prepared the performance copy of *A Christmas Carol.* The *Christmas Carol* performance copy, like the one for *The Cricket on the Hearth*, was more of a custom-made artifact than the subsequent performance texts, such as *David Copperfield.* Shortly after the late December 1853 performances of *A Christmas Carol*, Dickens arranged that the performance copy of his most famous Christmas story be assembled. This entailed hiring a book binder to detach the leaves from a copy of a standard

edition (Dickens chose the twelfth edition, 1849), and to paste them into windows that had been cut in larger blank leaves, and then to bind these composite leaves between marbled-paper boards. The binder then covered the spine and board corners in red, pebbled calfskin. The decorative design and color scheme may well reflect Dickens's instructions, since not only *A Christmas Carol* and *The Cricket on the Hearth* are bound in this manner, but so are all of the subsequently produced and heavily hand-emended and annotated performance copies, the texts of which were created in a very different manner, as we shall see. To aid him in his dramatic readings, he wrote words and phrases in the *Carol* performance copy, as he would in *David Copperfield* and in the margins of most of his performance copies, in order to remind himself of the tone he should adopt for certain passages of description, narration, or dialogue.

We find in the prompt copy of *A Christmas Carol* at least four principles that he followed in deleting and rewriting text, which he applied also to *David Copperfield*. First, complex sentences with dependent clauses were either deleted or rewritten more simply and concisely. Second, phrases that revealed characters' states of mind were almost always crossed out, since Dickens could convey them with his voice, facial expressions, and gestures. In this category we must include the deletion of scores of adjectives and adverbs. Third, Dickens often attempted to improve style, not merely compress the text. Finally, he deleted descriptive passages that created a mood, but did little to advance the narrative. In this category, in *A Christmas Carol*, we find some of Dickens's finest writing, the passages that give voice to the emotionally resonant descriptions of London's streets, weather, and varied inhabitants—many of them poor—as well as much of the dialogue between Scrooge and Marley's ghost and the Christmas Spirits, especially Scrooge's pleadings, often colored by a bleak, gallows humor. This last, sometimes neglected, quality of their conversations not only reveals the impact on Scrooge of the Christmas Spirits' visits, but endows Scrooge and the Spirits with a psychological complexity without which they would be little more than two-dimensional caricatures, instead of believable characters. But Dickens ruthlessly sacrificed most of these passages in the cause of creating a compact performance text, and in pursuit of another, programmatic, goal as well.

He wrote words and phrases in the margins to remind himself of the tone he should adopt.

THE SECOND OF THE THREE SPIRITS. 87

Scrooge promised that he would; and they went on, invisible, as they had been before, into the suburbs of the town. It was a remarkable quality of the Ghost (which Scrooge had observed at the baker's) that notwithstanding his gigantic size, he could accommodate himself to any place with ease; and that he stood beneath a low roof quite as gracefully and like a supernatural creature, as it was possible he could have done in any lofty hall.

And perhaps it was the pleasure the good Spirit had in showing off this power of his, or else it was his own kind, generous, hearty nature, and his sympathy with all poor men, that led him straight to Scrooge's clerk's; for there he went, and took Scrooge with him, holding to his robe; and on the threshold of the door the Spirit smiled, and stopped to bless Bob Cratchit's dwelling with the sprinklings of his torch. Think of that! Bob had but fifteen "Bob" a-week himself; he pocketed on Saturdays but fifteen copies of his Christian name; and yet the Ghost of Christmas Present blessed his four-roomed house!

Dickens's first editorial pass on this page of *A Christmas Carol* was in pencil, which reflects the changes he made at some point between the 1853 Birmingham reading (over three hours) and the 1857 London reading (two and a half hours); the second pass was in black ink (now turned brown); and the third, in blue ink.

In the book's published text, the Christmas-cheery passages, though only occasionally animated by Dickens's best writing, nevertheless effectively serve their purpose, which is to reassure the reader, by immersion in scenes of domestic happiness, perhaps more effective for being mundane and sentimental, that goodness is a refuge against evil, and may even, as with Scrooge, transform it. These scenes are effective, and their simple joys are so eagerly welcomed by readers, only because they have been driven into their embrace by the monstrous specter of Scrooge's cold, lonely heart; by the casual cruelty of the money-worshipping society he embodies; and by Scrooge's terror and guilt as he begins to see the suffering that he has inflicted both on himself and on others. Dickens's willingness to unbalance this finely modulated rhythm of horror and hope, this call and response of dark and light, could originate only in a motive as compelling to him now, in the late 1850s, as that which inspired the story's atmosphere of gloom and misery, in 1843. Dickens, whose childhood was blighted by deprivation and anxiety, and whose married life, by the early 1850s, was troubled, preferred, in performance, to emphasize the scenes depicting Christmas cheer and loving families. He found it more satisfying to share with a large audience seated expectantly before him his dreams of domestic bliss, rather than his stark knowledge of poverty, hunger, hopelessness, and the indifference of a cruel, selfish society. He also probably assumed that people would react more enthusiastically to, and be more likely to attend, a performance that was known to emphasize the bright and cheerful scenes at the expense of the most harrowing ones.

His audiences, unlike him, had no first-hand experience of poverty and the brutalizing, humiliating conditions in which the poor lived and worked.

Because of the admission prices for Dickens's readings, his audiences were predominantly wealthy, or at least comfortably middle class. He knew that they, unlike him, had no first-hand experience of poverty and the brutalizing, humiliating conditions in which the poor lived and worked. Though his audiences had been willing to learn about this world in the privacy of their parlors, reading Dickens's works silently, or perhaps reading aloud to each other, it was another matter entirely to have them pay an admission fee to a Christmas season extravaganza, and then listen to mortifying descriptions of hunger and abuse, and of the stark terror that Scrooge feels when he confronts his sinfulness and mortality. The ladies and gentlemen in attendance on those evenings had dressed in their finest clothes in order to enjoy themselves, not to be racked with fear and guilt.

In the *Christmas Carol* performance copy, we the see the evidence of Dickens's willingness to reshape what he had written to accommodate the needs of his own personality and purse. He would follow the same strategy in editing the performance copy of *David Copperfield.* But first he had to create a performance text. In contrast with the *Christmas Carol* and *Cricket* performance copies, for *Copperfield* and for the other performance copies, he submitted to the printer William Clowes and Sons a text that he had already radically compressed and edited, which was then printed in one or perhaps as many as three copies. One copy he would emend heavily in his own hand, and the others he probably kept at home in case the heavily emended copy should be lost; these he might lightly emend or leave clean. (The Berg Collection contains several of these lightly emended and clean performance copies.) The length of the *David Copperfield* text is perhaps one percent of that of the published text. Even the transcribed portions, divided into six chapters, have been compressed by about one-fifth. Dickens then subjected the printed text to an additional forty percent compression by hand, in at least two editorial passes, employing the same principles found in *A Christmas Carol* (as can be seen on page 80 of the Copperfield facsimile).

Of all his novels, **David Copperfield** *was his favorite, no doubt because he had modeled Copperfield's story so closely on his own.*

Dickens also rearranged one of his major excerpts for dramatic effect. Aside from this rearrangement of the narrative sequence, what immediately strikes the reader of the performance copy—and perhaps this was true as well for the first audiences that heard Dickens perform it—is the absence of any passages describing Copperfield's miserable experience in a bottling factory. Dickens famously said that of all his novels, *David Copperfield* was his favorite, and no doubt this was because he had modeled Copperfield's story so closely on his own. Dickens had been scarred by the humiliation and harsh treatment he

suffered as a twelve-year-old working in a boot polish factory to help support his family, which did not save his father from being sentenced to a debtor's prison and from the rest of the family, except for Charles, joining him there. For the *Copperfield* performance copy, Dickens chose to confine the excerpted and occasionally rewritten text to passages that describe the development of the novel's two primary love stories. The first involves Emily, the innocent, adored niece of Copperfield's sailor-friend, Mr. Peggotty. She falls in love with Copperfield's dashing school mate, Steerforth, who steals Emily from her fiancé cousin, Ham, and then abandons her. The second love story stars Copperfield and Dora, the sweet but childishly impractical woman whom Copperfield marries and lives with somewhat unhappily, until her premature death.

Excerpting passages from about a dozen chapters between Chapter 3 and Chapter 55 of the published version, Dickens's first two performance copy chapters tell the story of Copperfield bringing Steerforth to Peggotty's home (an old ship), where he meets Emily, and, in Chapter 2, of Copperfield returning to the ship, alone, to celebrate Emily's engagement to her cousin, only to hear the cousin himself announce the heart-rending news that Emily has run off with Steerforth. Chapter 3, in which Copperfield sets forth his relationship with Dora, and the dinner he gave for the Micawbers and Traddles, occurs in the published version prior to Copperfield's return to Peggotty's home and Emily's running away with Steerforth. It is clear that Dickens rearranged the novel's order so that the foreboding atmosphere of the Emily-Steerforth episodes might be relieved somewhat by the lighter tone of the Dora-Copperfield relationship. The performance text concludes with excerpts from Chapter 55, titled, in the published version, "The Tempest." That chapter, including the portions of it that Dickens excerpted for performance, contains some of the best and most frightening descriptions of stormy seas written in English. Yet Dickens crossed out much of it in his performance copy.

Dickens rearranged the novel's order so that the foreboding atmosphere might be relieved somewhat.

As in the *Christmas Carol* performance copies, Dickens crossed out passages in the *David Copperfield* performance copy that, on reflection, he thought might be too unpleasant for performance. We find, for example, on page 11 of his performance copy, that Dickens has deleted Peggotty's telling Copperfield how he felt when he discovered that Emily had run away with Steerforth: "I pray my good and gracious God to kill her (her that is so dear above all things) sooner than let her come to ruin and disgrace!" Dickens follows the same strategy when, on page 85, he deletes Peggotty's threat against Steerforth, following the words, "Let him never come nigh me." Dickens had originally written and faithfully excerpted, "I don't know what hurt I might do him." But he has crossed it out in the performance copy. These kinds of deletions weaken the power of Peggotty's narrative and turn Peggotty into a plaster saint, instead of showing him as the rough but compassionate sailor that Dickens had originally created. Peggotty's arduous wanderings in search of Emily become less meaningful to us, if we do not believe that he had to struggle against his violent anger.

Equally telling is Dickens's crossing out some of the most dramatic depictions of the tempest and its ravaging effect.

Equally telling is Dickens's crossing out in the performance copy some of the most dramatic depictions of the tempest and its ravaging effect on Ipswich and its inhabitants. To have retained even a few of these passages would have given the concluding portion of the performance text an intensity that would crescendo like one of the great breakers that Dickens describes, and that would then quietly subside into the elegiac denouement of Steerforth lying dead on the beach at Copperfield's feet. For instance, when Copperfield arrives at the beach to see a ship foundering in the storm, he comes upon a cluster of the town's terrified inhabitants (pages 90-92) "who had risen from their beds in the night, fearful of falling chimneys. Some of these told us of great sheets of lead having been ripped off a high church tower and flung into a bye-street. Others had to tell of country people, coming in from neighbouring villages, who had seen great trees lying torn out of the earth[...] When we came within sight of the sea, the waves on the horizon, seen at intervals above the rolling abyss, were like glimpses of another shore with towers and buildings.[...] As the receding wave swept back with a hoarse roar it seemed to scoop out deep caves in the beach.[...] Undulating hills were changed to valleys; undulating valleys were lifted up to hills; masses of water shivered and shook the beach with a booming sound; every shape rolled on, as soon as made, to change its shape and place,

and beat another shape and place away[...]." Dickens crossed out this entire, magnificent passage.

Several pages later (page 98), in another deleted passage, Dickens, through Copperfield's eyes, compares the ship in its death throes to "a desperate creature driven mad, now showing us the whole sweep of her deck, as she turned on her beam-ends towards the shore, now nothing but her keel as she sprung wildly over and turned towards the sea[...]." The reaction of the townspeople to the loss of the man who had been on board (Steerforth, as it happens), and of Ham, the jilted fiancé who had swum out to save him, is mortifying (bottom of page 98-page 99): "The agony on shore increased. Men groaned, and clasped their hands; women shrieked, and turned away their faces. Some ran wildly up and down, crying for help where no help could be." The deleted passages cited here, as well as others, which convey the grimmest, bleakest perspectives on the natural world and on human relations, Dickens crossed out, though he had them printed in the performance text. They are not sufficient in their length to have added much time to the performance, and in any case, there are many more mundane passages, as is the case in the *Christmas Carol* prompt copy, that could have been deleted in their place. But these deletions conform to Dickens's performance strategy of softening the more disturbing aspects of his work.

We can find in Dickens's performance books the impulse to please, which is the mark of the entertainer.

F. R. Leavis, the leading critic of the school of so-called "New Criticism" that arose in the 1930s, refused, for most of his career, to regard Dickens as a novelist worthy of being included in the canon of English literature. He notoriously claimed: "The adult mind doesn't as a rule find in Dickens a challenge to an unusual and sustained seriousness." He ranked Dickens among the great literary entertainers, not artists. This was a view that dominated serious literary criticism until the early 1950s. Though few would now make such a claim or deny that an artist may also entertain, we can find in Dickens's performance books the impulse to please, which is the mark of the entertainer, rather than to remain faithful to the truth of his creative impulse, no matter how disturbing, which is the mark of the artist. And yet these performance books rightly fascinate us because, regardless of Dickens's motives, these marked-up pages bring us in intimate contact with the vital imagination of a great writer, and with the good heart of a wise friend and guide, as he reworks his art to please us, performing before us on the page.

Isaac Gewirtz

Curator of the Henry W. and Albert A. Berg Collection
of English and American Literature
The New York Public Library

A Few Notes on Dickens's Notes

ON THE pages of his prompt copy where Dickens made changes by hand, we have transcribed these notes close to where he wrote them. These transcriptions are in upper- and lowercase letters. Dickens also wrote in some speaking cues to himself—the margin notes such as *Low, Sprightly laugh, Quick.* All of these are transcribed in SMALL CAPITAL LETTERS, to distinguish them from Dickens's changes to the narrative.

On many of the pages, Dickens wrote *stet* in the margin. This meant the crossed-out text should remain as it was originally typeset. The symbol ∂ indicates a deletion. *N.P.* on page 47 of the prompt copy indicates New Paragraph.

On page 81 of the prompt copy, Dickens has crossed out the last sentence that begins, "And may my prayers go up to Heaven...." Since he did not, however, excise the remainder of that sentence on page 82 of the prompt copy, we have reinstated it. His excision of all of page 81 makes it difficult to follow the rest of the first paragraph on page 82. It's possible that, in performance, Dickens may have inserted a brief phrase here, such as "...and Emily was found on the shore by a kind woman who took her in."

In a number of instances where Dickens was connecting two previously unjoined sentences, he neglected to change the period to a comma at the end of the first sentence, or to lowercase the first letter of the first word in the second sentence. In the transcription of the emended copy, we have silently corrected these minor oversights and made a few other adjustments to punctuation, where needed for clarity.

EX LIBRIS
CORTLANDT F. BISHOP
CHARLES DICKENS.

DAVID COPPERFIELD.

A Reading.

IN FIVE CHAPTERS.

PRIVATELY PRINTED

I had known the odd dwelling house inhabited by Mr Peggotty

In all, six chapters.

INTRODUCTION

TO

DAVID COPPERFIELD.

I had known Mr. Peggotty's house very well in my childhood, and if it had been Aladdin's palace, roc's egg and all, ~~I could not have been more charmed with it.~~ It was an old black barge or boat, high and dry on Yarmouth Sands, with an iron funnel sticking out of it for a chimney. There was a ~~delightful~~ door cut in the side, and it was roofed in, and there were little windows in it. It was beautifully clean and as tidy as possible. There wer some lockers and boxes, and there was a table, and there was a Dutch clock, and there was a chest of drawers, and there was a tea-tray with a painting or it, and the tray was kept from tumbling down, by a Bible; and the tray, if it *had* tumbled down, would

B

I am sure I could not have been more charmed with it.

have smashed a quantity of cups and saucers and a teapot that were grouped around the book. On the walls were coloured pictures of Abraham in red going to sacrifice Isaac in blue; and of Daniel in yellow being cast into a den of green lions. Over the little mantel-shelf was a picture of the 'Sarah Jane' lugger built at Sunderland, with a real little wooden stern stuck on it—a work of art combining composition with carpentry, which I had regarded in my childhood, as one of the most enviable possessions the world could afford. Mr. Peggotty, as honest a seafaring man as ever breathed, dealt in lobsters, crabs, and crawfish; and a heap of those creatures, in a state of wonderful conglomeration with one another and never leaving off pinching whatever they laid hold of, were usually to be found in a little wooden outhouse where the pots and kettles were kept.

As in my childhood, so in these days when I was a young man, Mr. Peggotty's household consisted of HIS ORPHAN NEPHEW HAM PEGGOTTY; HIS ADOPTED NIECE LITTLE EMILY, ONCE MY SMALL SWEETHEART,

a young Shipwright

a young shipwright

NOW A BEAUTIFUL YOUNG WOMAN; AND MRS. GUMMIDGE. All three had been maintained at Mr. Peggotty's sole charge for years and years; and Mrs. Gummidge was the widow of his partner in a boat, who had died poor. She was very grateful,

certainly   certainly   if she had not   if she had not

but she would have been more agreeable ~~company~~ ~~in a small habitation~~ if she had hit upon any other acknowledgment of the hospitality she received than constantly complain~~ed~~ing, as she sat in the most comfortable corner by the fireside, that she was "a lone lorn creetur and everythink went contrairy with her."

complained

Towards this old boat, I walked one memorable night, with my former schoolfellow and present dear friend, Steerforth; Steerforth, half a dozen years older than I; brilliant, handsome, easy, winning; whom I admired with my whole heart; for whom I entertained the most romantic feelings of fidelity and friendship. He had come down with me from

with the greatest ardour   with the greatest ardour

London, and had entered into my scheme of visiting the old simple place and the old simple people, ~~with the greatest ardour.~~

B 2

There was no moon; and as he and I walked on the dark wintry sands towards the old boat, the wind sighed mournfully ~~and a hoarse and solemn sound arose from the great deep.~~

"This is a wild place, Steerforth, is it not?"

"Dismal enough in the dark, and the sea ~~roars~~ has a cry in it, as if it were hungry for us. Is that the boat, where I see a light yonder?"

"That's the boat."

We said no more as we approached the light, but made softly for the door. I laid my hand upon the latch; and whispering Steerforth to keep close to me, went in.

A murmur of voices had been audible on the outside, and ~~at the moment of our entrance,~~ a clapping of hands: which latter noise, I was surprised to see, proceeded from the generally disconsolate Mrs. Gummidge. But Mrs. Gummidge was not the only person there, who was unusually excited. Mr. Peggotty, his face lighted up with uncommon satisfaction, held his ~~rough~~ arms wide open, as if for little Em'ly to run into them. Ham, ~~with a mixed~~

has a cry in it,

expression in his face of admiration, exultation, and a lumbering sort of bashfulness that sat upon him very well, held little Em'ly by the hand, as if he were presenting her to Mr. Peggotty; little Em'ly herself, blushing and shy, but delighted with Mr. Peggotty's delight, was stopped by our entrance (for she saw us first) in the very act of springing from Ham, to nestle in Mr. Peggotty's embrace. In the first glimpse we had of them all, and at the moment of our passing from the dark cold night into the warm light room, this was the way in which they were all employed.

The little picture was so instantaneously dissolved by our going in, that one might have doubted whether it had ever been. I was in the midst of the astonished family, face to face with Mr. Peggotty, and holding out my hand to him, when Ham shouted:

"Mas'r Davy! It's Mas'r Davy!"

In a moment we were all shaking hands with one another, and asking one another how we did, and telling one another how glad we were to meet, and

whom I had not seen from my childhood,

all talking at once. Mr. Peggotty was so ~~[illegible]~~ overjoyed to see me, and to see my friend, that he did not know what to say or do, but kept over and over again shaking hands with me, and then with Steerforth, and then with me, and then ruffling his shaggy hair all over his head, and [then] laughing with such glee and triumph, that it was a treat to see him.

"Why, that you two gentl'men — gentl'men growed—should come to this here roof to-night, of all nights in my life, is such a ~~thing~~ [merry-go-rounder] as never happened afore, I do rightly believe! Em'ly, my darling, come here! Come here, my little witch! Theer's Mas'r Davy's friend, my dear! Theer's the gentl'man as you've heerd on, Em'ly. He comes to see you, along with Mas'r Davy, on the brightest night of your uncle's life as ever was or will be, ~~Gorm the t'other one, and~~ horroar for it!"

~~Nobody in Mr. Peggotty's household had the least idea of the etymology of this word Gorm, but that they all considered it as most emphatic and expressive. After delivering his speech with extraordinary animation and pleasure, Mr. Peggotty~~

then

merry-go-rounder

put one of his large hands on each side of his niece's face, and kissing it a dozen times; laid it with a gentle pride and love upon his broad chest, and patted it as if his hand had been a lady's. Then he let her go; and as she ran into the little chamber where I used to sleep, looked round upon us, quite hot and out of breath with his uncommon satisfaction.

"If you two gentl'men—gentl'men growed now, and such gentl'men—" said Mr. Peggotty.

Ham cried: "So th' are, so th' are! Well said! So th' are. Mas'r Davy bor—gentl'men growed—so th' are!"

"If you two gentl'men, gentl'men growed, don't ex-cuse me for being in a state of mind, when you understand matters, I'll arks your pardon. Em'ly, my dear!—She knows I'm a going to tell, and has made off. Would you be so good as look arter her, Mawther, for a minute?"

Mrs. Gummidge nodded and disappeared.

"I'll pound it if this ain't," said Mr. Peggotty sitting down among us by the fire, "the brightest

her

Low

night of my life, and a reg'lar merry-go-rounder! This here little Em'ly, sir," in a low voice to Steerforth, "—her as you see a blushing here just now—

Steerforth only nodded; but with such a pleased expression of interest, and of participation in Mr. Peggotty's feelings, that Mr. Peggotty answered him as if he had spoken.

"To be sure. That's her, and so she is. Thankee, sir."

Ham nodded to me several times, as if he would have said so too.

"This here little Em'ly of ours, has been, in our house, sir, what I suppose (I'm a ignorant man, but that's my belief) no one but a little bright-eyed creetur *can* be in a house. She ain't my child; I never had one; but I couldn't love her more, if she was fifty times my child. You understand! I couldn't do it!"

"I quite understand," said Steerforth.

"I know you do, sir, and thankee again. Mas'r Davy, he can remember what she was; you may

Well sir. well sir.

judge for your own self what she is; but neither of you can't fully know what she has been, is, and will be, to my loving art. I am rough, sir, I am as rough as a Sea Porkypine; but no one, unless, may-hap, it is a woman, *can* know, I think, what our little Em'ly is to me."

Mr. Peggotty ruffled his hair again with both hands, as a further preparation for what he was going to say, and went on.

"There was a certain person as had know'd our Em'ly, from the time when her father was drownded; as had seen her constant; when a babby, when a young gal, when a woman. Not much of a person to look at, he warn't—something o' my own build—rough—a good deal o' the sou'-wester in him—wery salt—but, on the whole, a honest sort of a chap too, with his art in the right place."

[illegible] I had never seen Ham grin to anything like the extent to which he sat grinning at us now.

"What does this here blessed tarpaulin go and do, but he loses that there art of his to our little Em'ly. He follers her about, he makes hisself a sort o' servant to her, he loses in a great measure his relish for his wittles, and in the long run he makes it clear to me wot's amiss. Now I could wish myself, you see, that our little Em'ly was in a fair way of being married. I could wish to see her, at all ewents, under articles to a honest man as had a right to defend her. I doen't know how long I may live, or how soon I may die; but I know that if I was capsized, any night, in a gale of wind in our Roads here, and was to see the town-lights a shining for the last time over the rollers as I couldn't make no head against, I could go down quieter for thinking 'There's a man ashore there, iron-true to my little Em'ly, God bless her! and no wrong can touch my Em'ly while so be as that man lives!'

Mr. Peggotty, in simple earnestness, waved his arm, as if he were waving it at the town-lights for the last time, and then, exchanging a nod with Ham, whose eye he caught, proceeded as before.

'Well! I counsels him to speak to Em'ly. He's big enough, but he's bashfuller than a little un, and he says to me he doen't like. So *I* speak. 'What! *Him!*' says Em'ly. '*Him* that I've know'd so intimate so many year, and like so much! Oh, Uncle! I never can have *him*. He's such a good fellow!' I gives her a kiss, and I says no more to her than 'My dear, you're right to speak out, you're to choose for yourself, you're as free as a little bird.' Then I aways to him, and I says, 'I wish it could have been so, but it can't. But you can both be as you was, and wot I say to you is, Be as you was with her, like a man.' He says to me, a shaking of my hand, 'I will.!' he says. And he was—honourable, trew, and manful—going on for two year, and we was just the same at home here as afore.'

Mr. Peggotty's face, which had varied in its expression with the various stages of his narrative, now resumed all its former triumph and delight, as he laid a hand upon my knee and a hand upon Steerforth's (previously wetting them both, for the greater emphasis of the action), and divided the following speech between us:

"All of a sudden, one evening—as it might be to-night—comes little Em'ly from her work, and him with her! There ain't so much in *that*, you'll say. No, sure, because he takes care on her, like a brother, arter dark, and indeed afore dark, and at all times. But this heer tarpaulin chap, he takes hold of her hand, and he cries out to me, joyful, 'Lookee here! This is to be my little wife!' And she says, half bold and half shy, and half a laughing and half a crying, 'Yes, uncle! If you please.'—If I please! Lord, as if I should do anythink else!—'If you please,' she says, 'I am steadier now, and I have thought better of it, and I'll be as good a little wife as I can to him, for he's a dear good fellow!' Then Missis Gummidge, she claps her hands like a play, and you come in. There! The murder's out! You come in! It took place this here present hour; and here's the man as'll marry her, the minute she's out of her time at the needlework."

Ham staggered, as well he might, under the blow Mr. Peggotty dealt him, as a mark of confidence and friendship; but feeling called upon to say something to us, he stammered:

"She warn't no higher than you was, Mas'r Davy—when you first come heer—when I thought what she'd grow up to be. I see her grow up—gentl'men—like a flower. I'd lay down my life for her—Mas'r Davy—Oh! most content and cheerful! She's more to me—gentl'men—than—she's all to me that ever I can want, and more to me than ever I—than ever I could say. I—I love her trew. There ain't a gentl'man in all the land—nor yet a sailing upon all the sea—that can love his lady more than I love her, though there's many a common man—as could say better—what he meant."

I thought it affecting to see such a sturdy fellow trembling in the strength of what he felt for the pretty little creature who had won his heart. I thought the simple confidence reposed in us by Mr. Peggotty and by himself, was touching. I was affected by the story altogether. I was filled with pleasure by all this; but at first, with an indescribably sensitive pleasure, that a very little would have changed to pain.

Therefore, if it had depended upon me to touch the prevailing chord among them with any skill, I should have made a poor hand of it. But it depended upon Steerforth; and he did it with such address, that in a few minutes we were all as easy as possible.

"Mr. Peggotty," he said, "you are a thoroughly good fellow, and deserve to be as happy as you are to-night. My hand upon it! Ham, I give you joy, my boy. My hand upon that, too! Davy, stir the fire, and make it a brisk one! And Mr. Peggotty, unless you can induce your gentle niece to come back ~~(for whom I vacate this seat in the corner)~~, I shall go. Any gap at your fireside on such a night —such a gap least of all—I wouldn't make, for the wealth of the Indies!"

So, Mr. Peggotty went ~~into my old room~~ to fetch little Em'ly. At first little Em'ly didn't like to come, and then Ham went. Presently they brought her to the fireside, very much confused, and very shy,—but she soon became more assured when she found how ~~[illegible]~~ Steerforth spoke to her; how skilfully he avoided anything that would embarrass her; how he talked to Mr. Peggotty of boats, and ships, and tides, and fish; how delighted he was with that boat and all belonging to it; how lightly and easily he carried on, until he brought us, by degrees, into a charmed circle, and we were all talking away without reserve.

Em'ly, indeed, said little; but she looked, and listened, and her face got animated, and she was charming. Steerforth told a story of a shipwreck (which arose out of his talk with Mr. Peggotty) and little Em'ly's eyes were fastened on him all the time, as if she saw it. He told us a merry adventure of his own, as a relief—and little Em'ly laughed until the boat rang with the musical sounds. He got Mr. Peggotty to sing or rather to roar, "When the stormy winds do blow, do blow, do blow;" and he sang a sailor's song himself, so pathetically, that I could have almost fancied that the real wind creeping sorrowfully round the house, and murmuring low through our unbroken silence, was there to listen.

But he set up no monopoly of the conversation. He was silent and attentive when little Emily grew more courageous, and talked (but still bashfully) across the fire to me of our old childish wanderings upon the beach, to pick up shells and pebbles; he was silent and attentive also, when I asked her if she recollected how I used to love her, and how we used to walk about that dim old flat, in a loving manner, hours and hours, and how the days sported by us as if Time himself had not grown up then, but were a child like ourselves, and always at play. She sat all the evening on the old locker, in her old little corner by the fire—Ham beside her. I could not satisfy myself whether it was in her own little tormenting way, or in a maidenly reserve before us, that she kept quite close to the wall, and away from him; but I observed that she did so, all the evening.

very /

Ham

As I remember, it was almost midnight when we took our leave. We had had some biscuit and dried fish for supper, and Steerforth had produced from his pocket a flask of Hollands. We parted merrily; and as they all stood crowded round the door to light us on our road, I saw the sweet blue eyes of little Em'ly peeping after us, from behind Ham, and heard her soft voice calling to us to be careful how we went.

"A most engaging little Beauty!" said Steerforth, taking my arm. "Well! It's a quaint place, and they are quaint company; and it's quite a new sensation to mix with them."

Steerforth

"How fortunate we are, too, ~~I returned,~~ to have arrived to witness their happiness in that intended marriage! I never saw people so happy. How delightful to see it!" ~~and to be made the sharers of their honest joy, as we have been!"~~

"Yes—that's rather a chuckle-headed fellow for ~~the girl, isn't he?" said Steerforth.~~

the girl. Isn't he?"

I felt a shock in this ~~unexpected and~~ cold reply. But turning quickly upon him, and seeing a laugh in his eyes, I answered~~, much relieved~~:

"Ah, Steerforth! It's well for you to joke about the poor! But when I see how perfectly you understand them, and how you can enter into happiness like this plain fisherman's, I know there is not a joy, or sorrow, or any emotion, of such people, that can be indifferent to you.

c

And I admire and love you for it, Steerforth, twenty times the more!"

To my surprise, he cast down his eyes and became abstracted, and then suddenly said, with nothing, that I could see, to lead to it:

"Daisy, I wish to God I had had a judicious father these last twenty years!"

"My dear Steerforth, what is the matter?"

"You know my mother has always doted on me and spoilt me. I wish with all my soul I had been better guided! I wish with all my soul, I could guide myself better!"

There was a passionate dejection in his manner that quite amazed me. He was more unlike himself than I could have supposed possible.

"It would be better to be this poor Peggotty, or his lout of a nephew, than be myself, twenty times richer and twenty times wiser, and be the torment to myself that I have been in that Devil's bark of a boat within the last half-hour."

I was so confounded by the change in him that at first I could only regard him in silence as he walked at my side. At length I asked him, with all the earnestness I felt, to tell me what had happened to cross him so unusually, and to let me sympathize with him. Before I had well concluded, he began to laugh—fretfully at first, but soon with returning gaiety.

"Tut, it's nothing—nothing, Davy! I have been a nightmare to myself these last few minutes of our walk—must have had a nightmare, I think. At odd dull times nursery tales come up into the memory, unrecognized for what they are. I believe I have been confounding myself with the bad boy who 'didn't care' and became food for lions—a grander kind of going to the dogs, I suppose. What old women call the horrors, have been creeping over me from head to foot. I have been afraid of myself."

"You are afraid of nothing else, I think."

"Perhaps not, and yet may have enough to be afraid of, too. Well! so it goes by! Daisy—for though that's not the name your godfathers and godmothers gave you, you're such a fresh fellow that it's the name I best like to call you by—and I wish, I wish, I wish, you could give it to me!"

"Why, so I can, if I choose."

"Daisy, if anything should ever happen to separate us, you must think of me at my best, old boy. Come! let us make that bargain. Think of me at my best, if circumstances should ever part us!"

"You have no best to me, Steerforth, and no worst. You are always equally loved and cherished in my heart."

alone,

alone,

I was up, to go away next morning with the dawn, and, having dressed as quietly as I could, looked into his room. He was fast asleep; lying, easily, with his head upon his arm, as I had often seen him lie at school.

The time came in its season, and that was very soon, when I almost wondered that nothing troubled his repose, as I looked at him then. But he slept—let me think of him so again—as I had often seen him sleep at school; and thus, in this silent hour I left him.

—Never more, O God forgive you, Steerforth! to touch that passive hand in love and friendship. Never, never, more!

DAVID COPPERFIELD.

~~IN FIVE CHAPTERS.~~

CHAPTER THE ~~FIRST~~. Second

SECOND

~~I HAD known Mr. Peggotty's house very well in my childhood, and if it had been Aladdin's palace, roc's egg and all, I could not have been more charmed with it. It was an old black barge or boat, high and dry on Yarmouth Sands, with an iron funnel sticking out of it for a chimney, and smoking cosily. There was a delightful door cut in the side, and it was roofed in, and there were little windows in it. It was beautifully clean and as tidy as possible. There were some lockers and boxes, and there was a table, and there was a Dutch clock, and there was a chest of drawers, and there was a tea-tray with a painting on it representing a lady with a parasol taking a walk~~

again

B 2

Some months elapsed before I again found myself down in that part of the country, and approaching the old boat by night. ~~I remember the occasion well. Events of later date have floated from me to the shore where all forgotten things will re-appear; but this stands like a high rock in the Ocean.~~

Some months elapsed before I again found myself down in that part of the country, and approaching the old boat by night.

with a military-looking child who was trundling a hoop. The tray was kept from tumbling down, by a Bible; and the tray, if it *had* tumbled down, would have smashed a quantity of cups and saucers and a teapot that were grouped around the book. On the walls, ~~there~~ were coloured pictures of Abraham in red going to sacrifice Isaac in blue; and of Daniel in yellow being cast into a den of green lions. Over the little mantel-shelf was a picture of the 'Sarah Jane' lugger, built at Sunderland, with a real little wooden stern stuck on to it—a work of art combining composition with carpentry, which I had regarded as one of the most enviable possessions the world could afford. Mr. Peggotty, as honest a seafaring man as ever breathed, dealt in lobsters, crabs, and crawfish; and a heap of those creatures, in a state of wonderful conglomeration with one another and never leaving off pinching whatever they laid hold of, were usually to be found in a little wooden out-house where the pots and kettles were kept.

As in my childhood, so in these days when I

was a young man, Mr. Peggotty's household consisted of his orphan nephew Ham Peggotty; his adopted niece Little Emily, once my small sweetheart, now a beautiful young woman, on the eve of being married to Ham; and Mrs. Gummidge. All three had been maintained at Mr. Peggotty's sole charge for years and years; and Mrs. Gummidge was the widow of his partner in a boat, who had died poor. She was very grateful no doubt, but she would have been more agreeable company in a small habitation if she had hit upon any other acknowledgment of the hospitality she received than constantly complaining, as she sat in the most comfortable corner by the fireside, that she was "a lone lorn creetur and everythink went contrairy with her."

It was a dark evening, and rain was beginning to fall, when I came within sight of Mr. Peggotty's house, and of the light within it shining through the window. A little floundering across the sand, which was heavy, brought me to the door, and I went in.

I was bidden to a little supper; Emily was to be married to Ham that day fortnight, and this was the last time I was to see her in her maiden life.

the

I was bidden to a little supper; Emily was to be married to Ham that day fortnight, and this was the last time I was to see her in her maiden life.

It looked very comfortable, indeed. Mr. Peggotty had smoked his evening pipe, and there were preparations for some supper by-and-by. The fire was bright, the ashes were thrown up, the locker was ready for little Emily in her old place. In her own old place sat my dear old nurse, Mr. Peggotty's sister, looking as if she had never left it. Mrs. Gummidge appeared to be fretting a little, in her old corner; and consequently looked quite natural too.

own

"You're first of the lot, Mas'r Davy!" said Mr. Peggotty, with a happy face. "Doen't keep in that coat, sir, if it's wet."

"Thank you, Mr. Peggotty. It's quite dry."

"So 't is!" said Mr. Peggotty, feeling my shoulder. "As a chip! Sit ye down, sir. It ain't o' no use saying welcome to you, but you're welcome, kind and hearty."

"Thank you, Mr. Peggotty, I am sure of that. Well, dear old nurse," said I, giving her a kiss. "And how are you, old woman?"

Here Mrs. Gummidge groaned.

"Cheer up, my pretty mawther!" said Mr. Peggotty.

"No, no, Dan'l," returned Mrs. Gummidge. "Nothink's nat'ral to me but to be lone and lorn."

After looking at Mrs. Gummidge for some moments, in sore distress of mind, Mr. Peggotty glanced at the Dutch clock, rose, snuffed the candle, and put it in the window.

"Theer!" said Mr. Peggotty, cheerily. "Theer we are, Missis Gummidge!" Mrs. Gummidge slightly groaned again. "Lighted up, accordin' to custom! You're a wonderin' what that's fur, sir! Well, it's fur our little Em'ly. You see, the path ain't over light or cheerful arter dark; and when I'm here at the hour as she's a comin' home from her needlework down-town, I puts the light in the winder. That, you see, meets two objects. She says, says Em'ly, 'Theer's home!' she says. And likeways, says Em'ly, 'My uncle's theer!' Fur if I ain't theer, I never have no light showed.'

"You're a baby!" said his sister; very fond of him for it, if she thought so.

cheer up,
Mrs. Gummidge

with great
sympathy

It ain't o' no use
telling <u>me</u> to cheer
up, when everythink
goes contrairy with
me

Theer we are,
Mrs. Gummidge

to herself

You may say this
is like a Babby Sir

a babby in regard o' Em'ly.

"Well," returned Mr Peggotty, standing with his legs pretty wide apart, and rubbing his hands up and down them in his comfortable satisfaction, as he looked alternately at us and at the fire. "I doen't know but what I am a babby in regard o' Em'ly. Not, you see, to look at, but to—to consider on, you know. *I* doen't care, bless you! Now I tell you. When I go a looking and looking about that theer pritty house of our Em'ly's, all got ready for her to be married, almost immediate, to that there blessed Tarpaulin, our Ham, I'm—I'm Gormed—theer! I can't say no fairer—if I doen't feel as if the littlest things was her, a'most. I takes 'em up, and I puts 'em down, and I touches of 'em as delicate as if they was our Em'ly. So 't is with her little bonnets and that. I couldn't see one on 'em rough used a purpose—not fur the whole wureld. There's a babby fur you, in the form of a great Sea Porkypine!"

Mr. Peggotty relieved his earnestness with a roar of laughter. My old nurse and I both laughed, but not so loud.

"It's my opinion, you see," said Mr. Peggotty, with a delighted face, after some further rubbing of his legs, "as this is along of my havin' played with Em'ly so much when she was a child, and havin' made believe as we was Turks, and French, and sharks, and every wariety of forinners—bless you, yes; and lions and whales, and I don't know what all!—when she warn't no higher than my knee. I've got into the way on it, you know. Why, this here candle, now! *I* know wery well that arter she's married and gone, I shall put that candle theer, just the same as now. I know wery well that when I'm here o' nights (and where else should *I* live, bless your arts, whatever fortun' I come into!) and she ain't here, or I ain't theer, I shall put the candle in the winder, and sit afore the fire, pretending I'm expecting of her, like as I'm a doing now. If I don't believe it I'm a shell-fish—biled too, and I can't say fairer than that. *There's* a babby for you, in the form of a Sea Porkypine! Why, at the present minute, when I see the candle sparkle up, I says to myself,

'She's a looking at it! Em'ly's a coming!' *There's* a babby for you, in the form of a Sea Porkypine! Right too! ~~for all that," said Mr. Peggotty, stopping in his roar, and smiting his hands together; "~~ fur here ~~she~~ is!"

too!

No; it was only Ham. The night should have turned more wet since I came in, for he had a large sou'wester hat on, slouched over his face.

"Where's Em'ly?" ~~said Mr. Peggotty~~.

movement

Ham made a movement ~~motion with his head~~, as if she were outside. Mr. Peggotty took the light from the window, trimmed it, put it on the table, and was ~~busily~~ stirring the fire, when Ham, who had not moved, said:

"Mas'r Davy, will you come out a minute, and see what Em'ly and me has got to show you?"

~~We went out~~. As I passed him ~~at the door~~, I saw, to my astonishment and fright, that he was deadly pale. He ~~pushed me hastily into the open air, and~~ closed the door upon us. Only upon us two.

"Ham! What's the matter?"

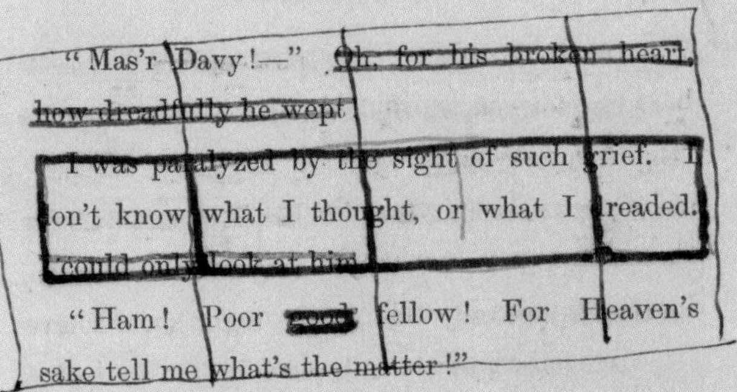

"Mas'r Davy!—" Oh, for his broken heart, how dreadfully he wept!

I was paralyzed by the sight of such grief. I don't know what I thought, or what I dreaded. I could only look at him.

"Ham! Poor good fellow! For Heaven's sake tell me what's the matter!"

"My love, Mas'r Davy—the pride and hope of my art—her that I'd have died for, and would die for now—she's gone!"

"Gone?"

"Em'ly's run away! Oh, Mas'r Davy, think *how* she's run away, when I pray my good and gracious God to kill her (her that is so dear above all things) sooner than let her come to ruin and disgrace!"

The face he turned up to the troubled sky, the quivering of his clasped hands, the agony of his figure, remain associated with that lonely waste in my remembrance, to this hour.

"You're a scholar, and know what's right and best. What am I to say, in-doors? How am I ever to break it to him, Mas'r Davy?"

I saw the door move, and ~~instinctively~~ tried to hold the latch ~~on the outside~~, to gain a moment's time. It was too late. Mr. Peggotty thrust forth his face; and never could I forget the change that came upon it when he saw us, if I were to live five hundred years.

an open letter

I remember a great wail and cry, and the women hanging about him, and we all standing in the room; I with ~~a paper~~ an open letter in my hand, which Ham had given me; Mr. Peggotty, with his vest torn open, his hair wild, his face and lips ~~quite~~ white, and blood trickling down his bosom (it had sprung from his mouth, I think)~~, looking fixedly at me~~.

"Read it, sir; slow, please. I doen't know as I can understand."

addressed to himself

In the midst of the silence of death, I read thus, from the blotted letter Ham had given me. In Emily's hand—addressed to himself—

"'When you, who love me so much better than I ever have deserved, even when my mind was innocent, see this, I shall be far away.'"

Stop! I shall be fur away," he repeated slowly.
"Stop! Em'ly fur away. Well!"
"'When I leave my dear home—my dear home—oh, my dear home!—in the morning,'"
—the letter bore date on the previous night:
"'—It will be never to come back, unless he brings me back a lady. This will be found at night, many hours after, instead of me. Oh, if you knew how my heart is torn. If even you, that I have wronged so much, that never can forgive me, could only know what I suffer! I am too wicked to write about myself. Oh, take comfort in thinking that I am so bad. Oh, for mercy's sake, tell uncle that I never loved him half so dear as now. Oh, don't remember how affectionate and kind you have all been to me—don't remember we were ever to be married—but try to think as if I died when I was little, and was buried somewhere. Pray Heaven that I am going away from, have compassion on my uncle! Tell him that I never loved him half so dear. Be his comfort. Love some good girl, that will be what I

don't

you and I

was once to uncle, and that will be true to you, and worthy of you, and know no shame but me. God bless all! I'll pray for all, often, on my knees. If he don't bring me back a lady, and I don't pray for my own self, I'll pray for all. My parting love to uncle. My last tears, and my last thanks, for uncle!'"

That was all.

He stood, long after I had ceased to read, still looking at me. At length I ventured to take his hand, and to entreat him, as well as I could, to endeavour to get some command of himself. He replied, "I thankee, sir, I thankee!" without moving.

Ham spoke to him. Mr. Peggotty was so far sensible of *his* affliction, that he wrung his hand; but, otherwise, he remained in the same state, and no one dared to disturb him.

Slowly, at last, he moved his eyes from my face, as if he were waking from a vision, and cast them round the room. Then he said, in a low voice:

"Who's the man? I want to know his name."

Ham glanced at me, and suddenly I felt a shock.

"There's a man suspected; who is it?"

"Mas'r Davy!" implored Ham. "Go out a bit, and let me tell him what I must. You doen't ought to hear it, sir."

I felt the shock again. I sank down in a chair, and tried to utter some reply; but my tongue was fettered, and my sight was weak. For I felt that the man was my friend—the friend I had unhappily introduced there—Steerforth, my old schoolfellow and my friend.

that the man

"I want to know his name!"

"For some time past," Ham faltered, "there's been a servant about here, at odd times. There's been a gen'lm'n too. Both of 'em belonged to one another."

Mr. Peggotty stood fixed as before, but now looking at him.

"The servant was seen along with—our poor girl—last night. He's been in hiding about here, this week or over. He was thought to have gone, but he was hiding. Doen't stay, Mas'r Davy, doen't!"

Doen't stay, Mas'r Davy, doen't!"

I could not have moved if the house had been about to fall upon me.

"A strange chay and horses was outside town, this morning, on the Norwich road, a'most afore the day broke. The servant went to it, and come from it, and went to it again. When he went to it again, Em'ly was nigh him. The t'other was inside, Mas'r Davy's frend. He's the man."

"For the Lord's love," said Mr. Peggotty, falling back, and putting out his hand, as if to keep off what he dreaded. "Doen't tell me his name's Steerforth!"

"Mas'r Davy," exclaimed Ham, in a broken voice, "it ain't no fault of yourn—and I am far from laying of it to you—but it is your friend Steerforth, and he's a damned villain!"

Mr. Peggotty uttered no cry, and shed no tear, and moved no more, until he seemed to wake again, all at once, and pulled down his rough coat from its peg in a corner.

"Bear a hand with this! I'm struck of a heap, and can't do it," he said, impatiently. "Bear a hand, and help me. Well!" when somebody had done so. " Now give me that theer hat!"

Ham asked him whither he was going?

"I'm a going to seek my niece. I'm a going to seek my Em'ly. I'm a going, first, to stave in that theer boat as he gave me, and sink it where I would have drownded *him*, as I'm a livin' soul, if I had had one thought of what was in him! As he sat afore me, in that boat," he said, wildly, holding out his clenched right hand, "as he sat afore me, face to face, strike me down dead, but I'd have drownded him, and thought it right!—I'm a going fur to seek my niece."

"Where?" cried Ham, interposing himself before the door.

"Anywhere! I'm a going to seek my niece through the wureld. I'm a going to find my poor niece in her shame, and bring her back wi' my comfort and forgiveness. No one stop me! I tell you I'm a going to seek my niece! I'm a going to seek her fur and wide!"

"No, no," Mrs. Gummidge, came between them,

in a fit of crying. "No, no, Dan'l, not as you are now. Seek her in a little while, my lone lorn Dan'l, and that'll be but right; but not as you are now. Sit ye down, and give me your forgiveness for having ever been a worrit to you, Dan'l —what have *my* contrairies ever been to this!— and let us speak a word about them times when she was first a orphan, and when Ham was too, and when I was a poor widder woman, and you took me in. It'll soften your poor heart, Dan'l, and you'll bear your sorrow better; for you know the promise, Dan'l, 'As you have done it unto one of the least of these, you have done it unto me;' and that can never fail under this roof, that's been our shelter for so many, many year!"

He was quite passive now; and when I heard him crying, the impulse that had been upon me to go down upon my knees, and ~~ask their pardon for the desolation I had innocently caused~~, and curse Steerforth, yielded to a better feeling. My overcharged heart found the same relief, as his and I cried too.

as his

CHAPTER III.

III.

At this period of my life I lived in my top set of chambers in Buckingham Street, Strand, London, and was over head and ears in love with Dora I lived principally on Dora and coffee. My appetite languished and I was glad of it, for I felt as though it would have been an act of perfidy towards Dora to have a natural relish for my dinner. I bought four sumptuous waistcoats —not for myself; *I* had no pride in them—for Dora. I took to wearing straw-coloured kid gloves in the streets. I laid the foundations of all the corns I have ever had. If the boots I wore at that period could only be produced and compared with the natural size of my feet, they would show in a most affecting manner what the state of my heart was.

C 2

housekeeper

Mrs. Crupp, the ~~laundress~~ of my chambers, must have been a woman of penetration; for, when this attachment was but a few weeks old, she found it out. She came up to me one evening when I was very low, to ask (being afflicted with spasms) if I could oblige her with a little tincture of cardamums, mixed with rhubarb and flavoured with seven drops of the essence of cloves—or, if I had not such a thing by me—with a little brandy. As I had never even heard of the first remedy, and always had the second in the closet, I gave Mrs. Crupp a glass of the second; which (that I might have no suspicion of its being devoted to any improper use) she began to take immediately.

she

"Cheer up, sir," said Mrs. Crupp. "Excuse me. I know what it is, sir. There's a lady in the case."

"Mrs. Crupp?"

"Oh, bless you! Keep a good heart, sir? Never say die, sir! If she don't smile upon you, there's a many as will. You're a young gentleman to *be* smiled on, Mr. Copperfull, and you must learn your walue, sir."

Mrs. Crupp always called me Mr. Copperfull: firstly, no doubt, because it was not my name; and secondly, I am inclined to think, in some indistinct association with a washing-day.

"What makes you suppose there is any young lady in the case, Mrs. Crupp?"

"Mr. Copperfull, said Mrs. Crupp, with a deal of feeling, 'I'm a mother myself. You don't eat enough, sir, nor yet drink.

"Is that what you found your supposition on, Mrs. Crupp?"

"Sir, I've laundressed other young gentlemen besides yourself. A young gentleman may be over-careful of himself, or he may be under-careful of himself. He may brush his hair too regular, or too unregular. He may wear his boots much too large for him, or much too small. That is according as the young gentleman has his nat'ral character formed. But let him go to which extreme he may, sir, there's a young lady in both of 'em."

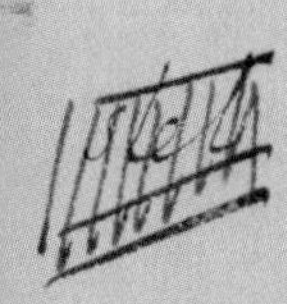

Your boots and your waist is equally very small, and

Mrs. Crupp shook her head in such a determined manner, that I had not an inch of 'vantage ground left.

"It was but the gentleman which died here before yourself, said Mrs. Crupp, that fell in love—with a barmaid—and had his waistcoats took in directly, though much swelled by drinking."

"Mrs. Crupp, said I, I must beg you not to connect the young lady in my case with a barmaid, or anything of that sort, if you please."

"Mr. Copperfull, I'm a mother myself, and not likely. I ask your pardon, sir, if I intrude. I should never wish to intrude where I were not welcome. But you are a young gentleman, Mr. Copperfull, and my adwice to you is, to cheer up, sir, to keep a good heart, and to know your own walue. If you was to take to something, sir; if you was to take to skittles, now, which is healthy, you might find it divert your mind, and do you good."

I turned it off and changed the subject by informing Mrs. Crupp that I wished to entertain

at dinner next day, my esteemed friend Traddles, and Mr. and Mrs. Micawber. And I took the liberty of suggesting a pair of soles, a small leg of mutton, and a pigeon pie. Mrs. Crupp broke out into rebellion on my first bashful hint in reference to her cooking the fish and joint, and terrified me by saying, "No! No, sir! You will not ask me sich a thing, for you are better acquainted with me than to suppose me capable of doing what I cannot do with ampial satisfaction to my own feelings!" But, in the end, a compromise was effected; and Mrs. Crupp consented to achieve this feat, on condition that I dined from home for a fortnight afterwards.

I bought a second-hand dumb-waiter for the dinner-party, in preference to re-engaging a handy young man who had waited on me before; against whom I had conceived a prejudice, in consequence of meeting him in the Strand, one Sunday morning, in a waistcoat remarkably like one of mine. A "young gal" whom I had previously employed on the motion of Mrs. Crupp

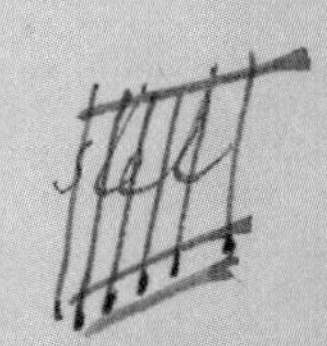

stet

was re-engaged; but on the stipulation that she should only bring in the dishes, and then withdraw to the landing-place, beyond the outer door; where a habit of sniffing she had contracted would be lost upon the guests.

Having laid in the materials for a bowl of punch, to be compounded by Mr. Micawber; having provided a bottle of lavender-water, two wax candles, a paper of mixed pins, and a pin-cushion, to assist Mrs. Micawber in her toilette, at my dressing-table; having also caused the fire in my bed-room to be lighted for Mrs. Micawber's convenience; and having laid the cloth with my own hands; I awaited the result with composure.

At the appointed time, my three visitors arrived together. Mr. Micawber with more shirt-collar than usual, and a new ribbon to his eye-glass; Mrs. Micawber with her cap in a whity-brown paper parcel; Traddles carrying the parcel, and supporting Mrs. Micawber on his arm. They were all delighted with my residence.

When I conducted Mrs. Micawber to my dressing-table, and she saw the scale on which it was prepared for her, she was in such raptures, that she called Mr. Micawber to come in and look.

"My dear Copperfield," said Mr. Micawber, "this is luxurious. This is a way of life which reminds me of the period when I was myself in a state of celibacy. I am at present established on what may be designated as a small and unassuming scale; but, you are aware that I have, in the course of my career, surmounted difficulties, and conquered obstacles. You are no stranger to the fact, that there have been periods of my life, when it has been requisite that I should pause, until certain expected events should turn up—when it has been necessary that I should fall back, before making what I trust I shall not be accused of presumption in terming—a spring. The present is one of those momentous stages in the life of man. You find me, fallen back, *for* a spring; and I have every reason to believe that a vigorous leap will shortly be the result."

~~To divert his thoughts,~~ I informed Mr. Micawber that I relied upon him for a bowl of punch, and led him to the lemons. I never saw a man so thoroughly enjoy himself ~~amid the fragrance of~~ lemon-peel and sugar, the odour of burning rum, and the steam of boiling water, as Mr. Micawber did that afternoon. It was wonderful to see his face shining at us out of a thin cloud of these delicate fumes, as he stirred, and mixed, and tasted, and looked as if he were making, not mere punch, but a fortune for his family down to the latest posterity. As to Mrs. Micawber, I don't know whether it was the effect of the cap, or the lavender-water, or the pins, or the fire, or the wax-candles, but she came out of my room, comparatively speaking, lovely. ~~And the lark was never gayer than that excellent woman.~~

I suppose—I never ventured to inquire, but I suppose—that Mrs. Crupp, after frying the soles, was taken ill. Because we broke down at that point. The leg of mutton came up, very red ~~within~~ and very pale ~~without~~ : besides having a

inside, outside

inside, outside

foreign substance of a gritty nature sprinkled over it, as if it had had a fall into ashes. But we were not in a condition to judge of this fact from the appearance of the gravy, forasmuch as ~~the "young gal" had dropped it all upon~~ the stairs. The pigeon-pie was not bad, but it was a delusive pie: the crust being like a disappointing head, ~~phrenologically speaking~~: full of lumps and bumps, with nothing particular underneath. In short, the banquet was such a failure that I should have been quite unhappy—about the failure, I mean, for I was always unhappy about Dora—if I had not been relieved by the great good-humour of my company.

it had been all dropped on

phrenological

"My dear friend Copperfield," said Mr. Micawber, "accidents will occur in the best-regulated families; and in families not regulated by that pervading influence which sanctifies while it enhances the—a—I would say, in short, by the influence of Woman in the lofty character of Wife, ~~they may be expected with confidence, and must be borne with philosophy.~~ If you will allow

especially

me to take the liberty of remarking that there are few comestibles better, in their way, than a Devil, and that I believe, with a little division of labour, we could accomplish a good one if the young person in attendance could produce a gridiron, I would put it to you, that this little misfortune may be easily repaired."

There was a gridiron in the pantry, on which my morning rasher of bacon was cooked. We had it out, in a twinkling, Traddles cut the mutton into slices; Mr. Micawber covered them with pepper, mustard, salt, and cayenne; I put them on the gridiron, turned them with a fork, and took them off, under Mr. Micawber's direction; and Mrs. Micawber heated ~~and continually stirred,~~ some mushroom ketchup in a little saucepan. ~~When we had slices enough done to begin upon, we fell-to, with our sleeves still tucked up at the wrists, more slices spluttering and blazing on the fire, and our attention divided between the mutton on our plates, and the mutton then preparing.~~ Under these circumstances,

Under these circumstances,

What with the novelty of this cookery, the excellence of it, the bustle of it, the frequent starting up to look after it, the frequent sitting down to dispose of it as the crisp slices came off the gridiron hot and hot, the being so busy, so flushed with the fire, so amused, and in the midst of such a tempting noise and savour, we reduced the leg of mutton to the bone. My own appetite came back miraculously. I am ashamed to record it, but I really believe I forgot Dora for a little while.

confess

TASTING

"Punch, my dear Copperfield," said Mr. Micawber, tasting it as soon as dinner was done, "like time and tide, waits for no man. Ah! it is at the present moment in high flavour. My love, will you give me your opinion?"

Mrs. Micawber pronounced it excellent.

"Then I will drink," said Mr. Micawber, "if my friend Copperfield will permit me to take that social liberty, to the days when my friend Copperfield and myself fought our way in the world side by side. I may say, of myself and Copperfield, in

words we have sung together before now—the words of the immortal exciseman nurtured beyond the Tweed—that

> We twa hae run about the braes
> And pu'd the gowans fine

—in a figurative point of view—on several occasions. I am not exactly aware what gowans may be, by-the-by, but I have no doubt that Copperfield and myself would frequently have taken a pull at them, if it had been feasible. My dear, another glass?"

Mrs. Micawber said it must be very little, but we couldn't allow that, so it was a glassful.

Sipping

SIPPING

" As we are quite confidential here, Mr. Copperfield," said Mrs. Micawber sipping her punch, " (Mr. Traddles being a part of our domesticity), I should much like to have your opinion on Mr. Micawber's prospects. I have consulted branches of my family on the course most expedient for Mr. Micawber to take, and it was, that he should immediately turn his attention to coals."

" To what, ma'am?"

"To coals. To the coal trade. Mr. Micawber was induced to think, on inquiry, that there might be an opening for a man of his talent in the Medway Coal Trade. Then, as Mr. Micawber very properly said, the first step to be taken clearly was, to go and *see* the Medway. Which we went and saw. I say 'we,' Mr. Copperfield; for I never will desert Mr. Micawber. I am a wife and mother, and I never will desert Mr. Micawber."

Traddles and I murmured our admiration.

"That," said Mrs. Micawber, "that, at least, is *my* view, my dear Mr. Copperfield and Mr. Traddles, of the obligation which I took upon myself when I repeated the irrevocable words 'I Emma, take thee, Wilkins.' I read the service over with a flat-candle, on the previous night, and the conclusion I derived from it was that I never could or would desert Mr. Micawber."

"My dear," said Mr. Micawber, a little impatiently, "I am not conscious that you are expected to do anything of the sort."

Traddles and I murmured our admiration and approbation of Mrs. Micawber.

"We went," repeated Mrs. Micawber, "and saw the Medway. My opinion of the coal trade on that river, was, that it might require talent, but that it certainly requires capital. Talent, Mr. Micawber has; capital, Mr. Micawber has not. We saw, I think, the greater part of the Medway; and that was my individual conclusion. My family were then of opinion that Mr. Micawber should turn his attention to corn—on commission. But corn, as I have repeatedly said to Mr. Micawber, may be gentlemanly, but it is not remunerative. Commission to the extent of two and ninepence in a fortnight cannot, however limited our ideas, be considered remunerative."

We were all agreed upon that.

"Then," said Mrs. Micawber, who prided herself on taking a clear view of things, and keeping Mr. Micawber straight by her woman's wisdom, when he might otherwise go a little crooked, "then I naturally look round the world, and say

'What is there in which a person of Mr. Micawber's talent is likely to succeed?' And I exclude doing anything on commission, because commission is not a certainty. What is best suited to a person of Mr. Micawber's peculiar temperament is, I am convinced, a certainty."

Traddles and I both expressed, by a feeling murmur, that this great discovery was no doubt true of Mr. Micawber, and that it did him infinite credit.

"I will not conceal from you, my dear Mr. Copperfield, that *I* have long felt the Brewing business to be particularly adapted to Mr. Micawber. Look at Barclay and Perkins! Look at Truman, Hanbury, and Buxton! It is on that extensive footing that Mr. Micawber, I know from my own knowledge of him, is calculated to shine; and the profits, I am told, are e-NOR—mous! But if Mr. Micawber cannot get into those firms—which decline to answer his letters, even when he offers his services in an inferior capacity—what is the use of dwelling upon that idea? None. I may have a conviction that Mr. Micawber's manners—"

"Hem! Really, my dear," interposed Mr. Micawber.

"My love, be silent. I may have a conviction, Mr. Copperfield, that Mr. Micawber's manners peculiarly qualify him for the Banking business. I may argue within myself, that if *I* had a deposit at a banking-house, the manners of Mr. Micawber, as representing that banking-house, would inspire confidence, and extend the connexion. But if the various banking-houses refuse to avail themselves of Mr. Micawber's abilities, or receive the offer of them with contumely, what is the use of dwelling upon *that* idea? None. As to originating a banking-business, I may know that there are members of my family who, if they chose to place their money in Mr. Micawber's hands, might found an establishment of that description. But if they do *not* choose to place their money in Mr. Micawber's hands—which they don't—what is the use of that? Again I contend that we are no farther advanced than we were before."

I shook my head, and said, "Not a bit." Traddles also shook his head, and said, "Not a bit."

"What do I deduce from this?" Mrs. Micawber went on to say, still with the same air of putting a case lucidly. "What is the conclusion, my dear Mr. Copperfield, to which I am irresistibly brought? Am I wrong in saying, it is clear that we must live?"

I answered, "Not at all!" and Traddles answered, "Not at all!" and I found myself afterwards sagely adding, alone, that a person must either live or die.

"Just so," returned Mrs. Micawber. "It is precisely that. Now I am convinced, myself, and this I have pointed out to Mr. Micawber several times of late, that things cannot be expected to turn up of themselves. We must in a measure, assist to turn them up. I may be wrong, but I have formed that opinion."

Both Traddles and I applauded it highly.

"Very well," said Mrs. Micawber. "Then what do I recommend? Here is Mr. Micawber with a variety of qualifications—with great talent—"

"Really, my love."

"Pray, my dear, allow me to conclude. Here is Mr. Micawber, with a variety of qualifications, with great talent—*I* should say, with genius, but that may be the partiality of a wife—"

Traddles and I both murmured "No."

"And here is Mr. Micawber without any suitable position or employment. Where does that responsibility rest? Clearly on society. Then I would make a fact so disgraceful known, and boldly challenge society to set it right. It appears to me, my dear Mr. Copperfield, that what Mr. Micawber has to do is to throw down the gauntlet to society, and say, in effect, 'Show me who will take that up. Let the party immediately step forward.'"

I ventured to ask Mrs. Micawber how this was to be done.

"By advertising in all the papers. It appears to me, that what Mr. Micawber has to do, in justice to himself, in justice to his family, and I will even go so far as to say in justice to society, by which he has been hitherto overlooked, is to advertise in all the papers; to describe himself plainly as so and so, with such and such qualifications, and to put it thus: '*Now* employ me, on remunerative terms, and address, post paid, to *W. M.*, Post Office, Camden Town.'"

"This idea of Mrs. Micawber's, my dear Copperfield," said Mr. Micawber, making his shirt-collar meet in front of his chin, and glancing at me sideways, "is, in fact, the Leap to which I alluded when I last had the pleasure of seeing you."

"Advertising is rather expensive," I remarked, dubiously.

"Exactly so!" said Mrs. Micawber, preserving the same logical air. "Quite true, my dear Mr. Copperfield! I have made the identical observation to Mr. Micawber. It is for that reason es-

For this purpose,

For this purpose, pecially, that I think Mr. Micawber ought (as I have already said, in justice to himself, in justice to his family, and in justice to society) to raise a certain sum of money—on a bill.

Mr. Micawber, leaning back in his chair, trifled with his eye-glass, and cast his eye up at the ceiling; but I thought him observant of Traddles, too, who was looking at the fire.

"If no member of my family," said Mrs. Micawber, "is possessed of sufficient natural feeling to negotiate that bill—I believe there is a better business-term to express what I mean—"

Mr. Micawber, with his eyes still cast up at the ceiling, suggested "Discount."

"To discount that bill, then, my opinion is, that Mr. Micawber should go into the City, should take that bill into the Money Market, and should dispose of it for what he can get. If the individuals in the Money Market oblige Mr. Micawber to sustain a great sacrifice, that is between themselves and their consciences. I view it, steadily, as an investment. I recommend Mr. Micawber,

, 40, and 41

my dear Mr. Copperfield, to do the same; to regard it as an investment which is sure of return, and to make up his mind to *any* sacrifice."

I felt, but I am sure I don't know why, that this was highly self-denying and devoted in Mrs. Micawber, and I uttered a murmur to that effect. Traddles, who took his tone from me, did likewise, and really I felt that she was a noble woman—the sort of woman who might have been a Roman matron, and done all manner of troublesome heroic public actions.

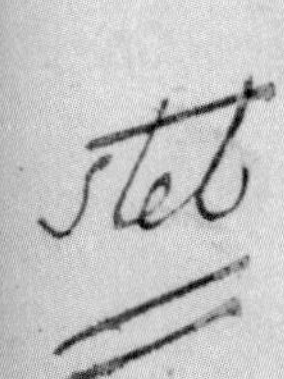

In the fervour of this impression, I congratulated Mr. Micawber on the treasure he possessed. So did Traddles. Mr. Micawber extended his hand to each of us in succession, and then covered his face with his pocket-handkerchief, which I think had more snuff upon it than he was aware of. He then returned to the punch, in the highest state of exhilaration.

He was full of eloquence. He gave us to understand that in our children we lived again, and that, under the pressure of pecuniary difficulties, any accession to their number was doubly welcome. He said that Mrs. Micawber had latterly had her doubts on this point, but that he had dispelled them, and reassured her. As to her family, they were totally unworthy of her, and their sentiments were utterly indifferent to him, and they might—I quote his own expression—go to the Devil.

Mr. Micawber then delivered a warm eulogy on Traddles. He said Traddles's was a character, to the steady virtues of which he (Mr. Micawber) could lay no claim, but which, he thanked Heaven, he could admire. He feelingly alluded to the young lady, unknown, whom Traddles had honoured with his affection, and who had reciprocated that affection by honouring and blessing Traddles with *her* affection. Mr. Micawber pledged her. So did I. Traddles thanked us both, by saying, with a simplicity and honesty I had sense enough to be quite charmed with, "I am very much obliged to you indeed. And I do assure you she's the dearest girl!"

Mr. Micawber took an early opportunity, after that, of hinting, with the utmost delicacy and ceremony at the state of *my* affections. Nothing but the serious assurance of his friend Copperfield to the contrary, he observed, could deprive him of the impression that his friend Copperfield loved and was beloved. After feeling very hot and uncomfortable for some time, and after a good deal of blushing, stammering, and denying, I said, having my glass in my hand, "Well! I would give them D.!" which so excited Mr. Micawber, that he ran with a glass of punch into my bed-room, in order that Mrs. Micawber might drink D., who drank it with enthusiasm, crying from within, in a shrill voice, "Hear, Hear! My dear Mr. Copperfield, I am delighted. Hear!" and tapping at the wall, by way of applause.

Mrs. Micawber made tea for us in a most agreeable manner; and, whenever I went near her, in handing about the teacups and bread-and-butter, asked me, in a whisper, whether D. was fair, or dark, or whether she was short, or tall: or some-

after Tea

thing of that kind; which I think I liked. After tea, we discussed a variety of topics before the fire; and Mrs. Micawber was good enough to sing us (in a small, thin, flat voice, which I remembered to have considered, when I first knew her, the very table-beer of acoustics) the favourite ballads of "The Dashing White Sergeant," and "Little Tafflin." For both of these songs Mrs. Micawber had been famous when she lived at home with her papa and mamma. Mr. Micawber told us, that when he heard her sing the first one, on the first occasion of his seeing her beneath the parental roof, she had attracted his attention in an extraordinary degree; but that when it came to Little Tafflin, he had resolved to win that woman or perish in the attempt.

She

she

stet

It was between ten and eleven o'clock when Mrs. Micawber rose to replace her cap in the parcel, and to put on her bonnet. Mr. Micawber took the opportunity of Traddles putting on his greatcoat, to slip a letter into my hand, with a whispered request that I would read it at my

stet

~~leisure.~~ I ~~also~~ took the opportunity of ~~my~~ holding a candle over the bannisters to light them down, when Mr. Micawber ~~was~~ going first, leading Mrs. Micawber, to detain Traddles for a moment on the top of the stairs.

"Traddles, Mr. Micawber don't mean any harm, ~~poor fellow~~; but, if I were you, I wouldn't lend him anything."

"My dear Copperfield, I haven't got anything to lend."

"You have got a name, you know."

"Oh! You call *that* something to lend?"

"Certainly."

"Oh! Yes, to be sure! I am very much obliged to you, Copperfield, but—I am afraid I have lent him that already."

"For the bill that is to ~~be a certain investment?~~" go into the money market

"No. Not for that one. This is the first I have heard of that one. I have been thinking that ~~he~~ will most likely propose that one, on the way home. Mine's another."

"I hope there will be nothing wrong about it."

"I hope not," said Traddles. "I should think not, though, because he told me, only the other day, that it was provided for. That was Mr. Micawber's expression, 'Provided for.'"

Mr. Micawber looking up at this juncture to where we were standing, I had only time to repeat my caution. Traddles thanked me, and descended. But I was much afraid, when I observed the good-natured manner in which he went down with Mrs. Micawber's cap in his hand, that he would be carried into the Money Market, neck and heels.

which

I returned to my fireside, and read Mr. Micawber's letter. It was dated an hour and a half before dinner. I am not sure whether I have mentioned that, when Mr. Micawber was at any particularly desperate crisis, he used a sort of legal phraseology: which he seemed to think equivalent to winding up his affairs.

stet

"Sir—for I dare not say my dear Copperfield,

"It is expedient that I should inform you that the undersigned is Crushed. Some flickering

This was the letter

efforts to spare you the premature knowledge of his calamitous position, you may observe in him this day; but hope has sunk beneath the horizon, and the undersigned is Crushed.

"The present communication is penned within the personal range (I cannot call it the society) of an individual, in a state closely bordering on intoxication, employed by a broker. That individual is in legal possession of the premises, under a distress for rent. His inventory includes, not only the chattels and effects of every description belonging to the undersigned, as yearly tenant of this habitation, but also those appertaining to Mr. Thomas Traddles, lodger, a member of the Honourable Society of the Inner Temple.

"If any drop of gloom were wanting in the overflowing cup, which is now 'commended' (in the language of an immortal Writer) to the lips of the undersigned, it would be found in the fact, that a friendly acceptance granted to the undersigned, by the before-mentioned Mr. Thomas Traddles, for the sum of £23 4*s*. 9½*d*. is over due,

Stet.

and is NOT provided for. Also, in the fact, that the living responsibilities clinging to the undersigned, will, in the course of nature be increased by the sum of one more helpless victim; whose miserable appearance may be looked for—in round numbers—at the expiration of a period not exceeding six lunar months from the present date.

"After premising thus much, it would be a work of supererogation to add, that dust and ashes are for ever scattered

"On

"The

"Head

"Of

"WILKINS MICAWBER."

Stet.

CHAPTER IV.

IV.

seldom

Seldom

did I wake at night, did I look up at the moon or stars or watch the falling rain, or hear the wind, but I thought of the solitary figure of the good fisherman toiling on—poor Pilgrim!—and recalled his words, "I'm a going to seek my niece. I'm a going to seek her fur and wide."

Months passed, and he had been absent—no one knew where—the whole time. It had been a bitter day, and a cutting north-east wind had blown. The wind had gone down with the light, and snow had come on

in London

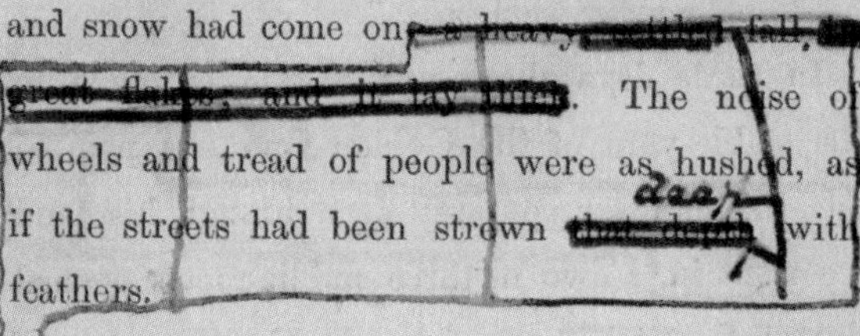

The noise of wheels and tread of people were as hushed, as if the streets had been strewn with feathers.

My shortest way home,—and I naturally took

the shortest way on such a night—was through Saint Martin's Lane. On the steps of the church, there was the stooping figure of a man, who had put down some burden on the smooth snow, to adjust it. I stood face to face with Mr. Peggotty! We shook hands. At first neither of us could speak a word.

And

"Mas'r Davy! It do my art good to see you, sir. Well met, well met!"

"Well met, my dear old friend!"

"I had thowts o' coming to make inquiration for you, sir, to-night, but it was too late. I should have come early in the morning, sir, afore going away agen."

"Again?"

"Yes, sir," he replied, patiently shaking his head, "I'm away to-morrow."

In those days there was a side entrance to the stable-yard of the Golden Cross. I pointed out the gateway, put my arm through his, and we went in. Two or three public-rooms opened out of the stable-yard; and looking into one of

Inn

them, and finding it empty, and a good fire burning, I took him in there.

When I saw him in the light, I observed, not only that his hair was long and ragged, but that his face was burnt dark by the sun. He was grayer, the lines in his face and forehead were deeper, and he had every appearance of having toiled and wandered through all varieties of weather; but he looked very strong, and like a man upheld by stedfastness of purpose, whom nothing could tire out. He shook the snow from his hat and clothes, and brushed it away from his face. As he sate down opposite to me at a table, with his back to the door by which we had entered, he put out his rough hand again, and grasped mine warmly.

"I'll tell you, Mas'r Davy, wheer-all I've been, and what-all we've heerd. I've been fur, and we've heerd little; but I'll tell you!"

I rang the bell for something hot to drink. He would have nothing stronger than ale; and while it was being brought, and being warmed

E

As

As ~~at the fire,~~ he sat thinking. There was a fine massive gravity in his face, which I did not venture to disturb.

You see, Sir—,

You see, Sir— "When she was a child, she used to talk to me a deal about the sea, and about them coasts where the sea got to be dark blue, and to lay a shining and a shining in the sun. I thowt, odd times, as her father being drownded, made her think on it so much. I doen't know, you see, but maybe she believed—or hoped—he had drifted out to them parts, where the flowers is always a blowing, and the country bright."

"It is likely to have been a childish fancy."

"When she was—lost, I know'd in my mind, as he would take her to them countries. I know'd in my mind, as he'd have told her wonders of 'em, and how she was to be a lady theer, and how he first got her to listen to him along o' sech like. I went across-channel to France, and landed theer, as if I'd fell down from the skies. I found out a English gentleman, as was in authority, and told him I was going to seek my niece. He got me them papers as I wanted fur to carry me through—I doen't rightly know how they're called—and he would have give me money, but that I was thankful to have no need on. I thank him kind, for all he done, I'm sure! I told him, best as I was able, what my gratitoode was, and went away through France, fur to seek my niece."

"Alone, and on foot?"

"Mostly a-foot; sometimes in carts along with people going to market; sometimes in empty coaches. Many mile a day a-foot, and often with some poor soldier or another, travelling fur to see his friends. I couldn't talk to him, nor he to me; but we was company for one another, too, along the dusty roads. When I come to any town, I found the inn, and waited about the yard till some one came by (some one mostly did) as know'd English. Then I told how that I was on my way to seek my niece, and they told me what manner of gentlefolks was in the house, and I waited to see any as seemed like her, going in or out. When it warn't Em'ly, I went on agen. By little and little, when I come to a new village or that, among the poor people, I found they know'd about me. They would set me down at their cottage doors, and give me what-not fur to eat and drink, and show me where to sleep. And many a woman, Mas'r Davy, as has had a daughter of about Em'ly's age, I've found a-waiting for me, at Our Saviour's Cross outside the village, fur to do me sim'lar kindnesses. Some has had daughters as was dead. And God only knows how good them mothers was to me! They would often put their children—partic'lar their little girls—upon my knee; and many a time you might have seen me sitting at their doors, when night was coming on, a'most as if they'd been my Darling's children. Oh, my Darling!"

I laid my trembling hand upon the hand he put before his face. "Thankee, sir, doen't take no notice."

"At last I come to the sea. It warn't hard, you may suppose, for a seafaring man like me to work his way over to Italy. When I got theer, I wandered on as I had done afore. I got news of her being seen among them Swiss mountains yonder. One as know'd his servant see 'em theer, all three, and told me how they travelled, and wheer they was. I made for them mountains, Mas'r Davy, day and night. Ever so fur as I went, ever so fur them mountains seemed to shift away from me. But I come up with 'em, and I crossed 'em. When I got nigh the place as I had been told of, I began to think within my own self, 'What shall I do when I see her?' I never doubted her. No! Not a bit! On'y let her see my face—on'y let her heer my voice—on'y let my stanning still afore her bring to her thoughts the home she had fled away from, and the child she had been—and if she had growed to be a royal lady, she'd have fell down at my feet! I know'd it well! Many a time in my sleep had I heerd her cry out, 'Uncle!' and seen her fall like death afore me. Many a time in my sleep had I raised her up, and whispered to her, Em'ly, my dear, I am come fur to bring forgiveness, and to take you home!' Well! He was nowt to me now. Em'ly was all. I bought a country dress to put upon her. To put that dress upon her, and to cast off what she wore—to take her on my arm again, and wander towards home—to stop sometimes upon the road, and heal her bruised feet and her worse-bruised heart—was all I thowt of now. But, Mas'r Davy, it warn't to be—not yet! I was too late, and they was gone. Wheer, I couldn't learn. Some said heer, some said theer. I travelled heer, and I travelled theer, but I found no Em'ly, and I travelled home."

"How long ago?"

"A matter o' fower days. I sighted the old boat arter dark, and the light a shining in the winder. When I come nigh and looked in through the glass, I see the faithful creetur Missis Gummidge a sittin' by the fire, as she and me had fixed upon, alone. I called out, 'Doen't be afeerd! It's Dan'l!' and I went in. I never

, I'm sure, that

could have thowt the old boat would have been so strange!"

From some pocket in his breast, he took out with a very careful hand, a small paper bundle containing two or three letters or little packets, which he laid upon the table.

The faithful creetur Mrs Gummidge gave me these

"This first one come afore I had been gone a week. A fifty pound Bank note, in a sheet of paper, directed to me, and put underneath the door in the night. She tried to hide her writing, but she couldn't hide it from Me! This one come to Missis Gummidge, two or three months ago. Five pounds."

It was untouched like the previous sum, and he refolded both.

"Is that another letter in your hand?"

"It's money too, sir. Ten pound, you see. And wrote inside, 'From a true friend.' But the two first was put underneath the door, and this come by the post, day afore yesterday. I'm going to seek her at the post-mark."

He showed it to me. It was a town on the

Upper Rhine. He had found out, at Yarmouth, some foreign dealers who knew that country, and they had drawn him a rude map on paper, which he could very well understand.

I asked him how Ham was? ~~He shook his head~~.

"He works as bold as a man can. ~~His name's as good, in all that part, as any man's is, anywheres in the wureld. Anyone's hand is ready to help him, you understand, and he is ready to help them.~~ He's never been heerd fur to complain. But my [illegible] belief is ('twixt ourselves) as it has cut him deep. Well! Having seen you to-night, Mas'r Davy (and that doos me good!), I shall away betimes to-morrow morning. You have seen what I've got heer;" putting his hand on where the little packet lay; "all that troubles me is, to think that any harm might come to me, afore this money was give back. If I was to die, and it was lost, or stole, or elseways made away with, and it was never know'd by him but what I'd ~~took~~ it, I believe the t'other wureld wouldn't hold me! I believe I must come back!"

accepted of

He rose, and I rose too. We grasped each other by the hand again, and as we went out into the rigorous night, everything seemed to be hushed in reverence for him, when he resumed his solitary journey through the snow.

V.

CHAPTER IV.

ALL this time I had gone on loving Dora harder than ever. If I may so express it, I was steeped in Dora. I was not merely over head and ears in love with her; I was saturated through and through. I took night walks to Norwood where she lived, and perambulated round and round the house and garden for hours together; looking through crevices in the palings, using violent exertions to get my chin above the rusty nails on the top, blowing kisses at the lights in the windows, and romantically calling on the night to shield my Dora. I don't exactly know from what —I suppose from fire—perhaps from mice, to which she had a great objection.

discreet

Dora had a discreet friend, comparatively stricken in years—almost of the ripe age of twenty, I should

—whose

say, her name was Miss Mills, and Dora called

~~&~~,

her Julia. She was the bosom friend of Dora. Happy Miss Mills!

One day Miss Mills said, "Dora is coming to stay with me. She is coming the day after to-morrow. If you would like to call, I am sure papa would be happy to see you." What could I do but invoke a silent blessing on Miss Mills's head, and store Miss Mills's address in the securest corner of my memory?

I passed three days in a luxury of wretchedness, torturing myself by putting every conceivable variety of discouraging construction on all that had ever taken place between Dora and me. At

and

last, arrayed for the purpose at a vast expense, I went to Miss Mills's fraught with a declaration.

Mr. Mills was not at home. I didn't expect he would be. Nobody wanted *him*. Miss Mills was at home. Miss Mills would do.

I was shown into a room up-stairs, where Miss Mills and Dora were. Dora's little dog Jip was there. Miss Mills was copying music, and Dora was painting flowers. What were my feelings when I recognized flowers I had given her! I cannot say that they were very like, or that they particularly resembled any flowers that have ever come under my observation.

Miss Mills was very glad to see me, and very sorry her papa was not at home: though I thought we all bore that with fortitude. Miss Mills was conversational for a few minutes, and then, laying down her pen, got up and left the room.

I began to think I would put it off till to-morrow.

"I hope your poor horse was not tired, when he got home at night from that pic-nic," said Dora, lifting up her beautiful eyes. "It was a long way for him."

I began to think I would do it to-day.

"It was a long way for *him*, for *he* had nothing to uphold him on the journey."

"Wasn't he fed, poor thing?" asked Dora.

I began to think I would put it off till to-morrow.

"Ye—yes, he was well taken care of. I mean he had not the unutterable happiness that I had in being so near you."

Dora bent her head over her drawing, and said, after a little while—I had sat, in the interval, in a burning fever, and with my legs in a very rigid state—

"You didn't seem to be sensible of that happiness yourself, at one time of the day."

I saw now that I was in for it, and it must be done on the spot.

"You didn't care for that happiness in the least," said Dora, slightly raising her eyebrows and shaking her head, "when you were sitting by Miss Kitt."

Kitt I should observe, was the name of a feminine creature in pink, with little eyes, with whom I had flirted at the pic-nic in madness and despair.

"Though certainly I don't know why you should care for being near me," said Dora, "or why you should call it a happiness at all. But of course you don't mean what you say. And I am sure no one doubts your being at liberty to do whatever you like. Jip, you naughty boy, come here!"

but

I don't know how I did it, but I did it in a moment. I intercepted Jip. I had Dora in my arms. I was full of eloquence. I never stopped for a word. I told her how I loved her. I told her I should die without her. I told her that I idolized and worshipped her. Jip barked madly all the time.

My

When Dora hung her head and cried and trembled, my eloquence increased so much the more and

and

I said, if she would like me to die for her, she had but to say the word, and I was ready. Life without Dora's love was not a thing to have on any terms. I couldn't bear it, and I wouldn't. I had

to distraction

loved her to distraction every minute, day and night, since I

set eyes upon

first set eyes upon saw her. I loved her at that minute to distraction. I should always love her, every minute, to distraction. Lovers had loved before, and lovers would love again; but no lover had ever loved, might, could, would, or should, ever love, as I loved Dora. The more I raved, the more Jip barked. Each of us, in his own way, got more mad every moment.

Well, well! Dora and I were sitting on the sofa by-and-by, quiet enough, and Jip was lying in her lap, winking peacefully at me. It was off my mind. I was in a state of perfect rapture. Dora and I were engaged.

Being poor, I felt it necessary the next time I went to my darling, to expatiate on that unfortunate drawback. I soon carried desolation into the bosom of our joys—not that I meant to do it, but that I was so full of the subject—by asking Dora, without the smallest preparation, if she could love a beggar?

My pretty, little, startled Dora! Her only association with the word was a yellow face and a nightcap, or a pair of crutches, or a wooden leg, or a dog with a decanter-stand in his mouth, or something of that kind; and she stared at me with the most delightful wonder.

Sprightly laugh

SPRIGHTLY LAUGH

"How can you ask me anything so foolish? Love a beggar!"

"Dora, my own dearest! *I* am a beggar!"

"How can you be such a silly thing," replied Dora, slapping my hand, "as to sit there, telling such stories? I'll make Jip bite you!"

"Dora, my own life, I am your ruined David!"

"I declare I'll make Jip bite you!" said Dora, shaking her curls, "if you are so ridiculous."

But I looked so serious, that Dora left off shaking her curls, and laid her trembling little hand upon my shoulder, and first looked scared and anxious, then began to cry. That was dreadful. For some time, poor little Dora did nothing but exclaim Oh dear! Oh dear! And oh, she was so frightened! And where was Julia Mills! And oh, take her to Julia Mills, and go away, please! until I was almost beside myself.

She

I thought I had killed her. I sprinkled water on her face. I went down on my knees. I plucked at my hair. I denounced myself as a remorseless brute, and beast. I implored her forgiveness. I besought her to look up. I ravaged Miss Mills's work-box for a smelling-bottle, and in my agony of mind applied an ivory needle-case instead, and dropped all the needles over Dora. I shook my fists at Jip, who was as frantic as myself. I did every wild extravagance that could be done.

At last, after an agony of supplication, I got Dora to look at me, with a horrified expression of face, which I gradually soothed until it was only loving, and her soft, pretty cheek was lying against mine.

"Is your heart mine still, dear Dora?" said I, rapturously, for I knew by her clinging to me that it was.

"Oh, yes!" cried Dora. "Oh, yes, it's all yours. Oh, don't be dreadful!"

I dreadful. To Dora!

"Don't talk about being poor, and working hard! Oh, don't, don't!"

"My dearest love, the crust well-earned—"

"Oh, yes; but I don't want to hear any more

F

after we are married,

after we are married,

about crusts! And Jip must have a mutton-chop every day at twelve, or he'll die!"

I was charmed with her childish, winning way, and I fondly explained to her that Jip should have his mutton-chop with his accustomed regularity.

One thing troubled me though, after we had fallen into a quiet train and were in a fair way to be married. It was, that Dora seemed by one consent to be regarded like a pretty toy or plaything. It was very odd to me; but they all seemed to treat Dora, in her degree, much as Dora treated Jip in his.

I made up my mind to speak to Dora about this; and one day, I said to her that I wished she could get them to behave towards her differently.

"Because you know, my darling, you are not a child."

"There! Now you're going to be cross!"

"Cross, my love?"

"I am sure they're very kind to me, and I am very happy."

"Well! But my dearest life, you might be very happy, and yet be treated rationally."

Dora gave me a reproachful look—the prettiest look!—and then began to sob, saying if I didn't like her, why had I ever wanted so much to be engaged to her? And why didn't I go away now, if I couldn't bear her?

What could I do but kiss away her tears, and tell her how I doted on her, after that!

~~I was charmed by her presently asking me, of her own accord,~~ to give her that cookery-book I had once spoken of, and to show her how to keep accounts, as I had once promised I would. I brought the volume with me on my next visit (I got it prettily bound, first, to make it look less dry and more inviting); and showed her an old house-keeping-book of my aunt's, and gave her a set of tablets, and a pretty little pencil-case, and a box of leads, to practise house-keeping with.

But the cookery-book made Dora's head ache, and the figures made her cry. They wouldn't add up, she said. So she rubbed them out, and drew

F 2

When we had been engaged some half a year or so, Dora delighted me by asking me

housekeeping

little nosegays, and likenesses of me and Jip, all over the tablets.

Then I playfully tried verbal instruction in domestic matters. Sometimes, for example, when we passed a butcher's shop, I would say:

"Now suppose, my pet, that we were married, and you were going to buy a shoulder of mutton for dinner, would you know how to buy it?"

My pretty little Dora's face would fall, and she would make her mouth into a rosebud, as if she would very much prefer to shut mine with a kiss.

"Would you know how to buy it, my darling?" I would repeat, if I were very inflexible.

Dora would think a little, and would then reply with great triumph:

"Why, the butcher would know how to sell it, and what need *I* know? Oh, you silly boy!"

So, when I once asked Dora, with an eye to the cookery-book, what she would do, if we were married, and I were to say I should like a nice Irish stew, she replied that she would tell the servant to make it; and then clapped her little hands together across my arm, and laughed in such a charming manner that she was more delightful than ever.

Time went on, and at last, here in this hand of mine I held the wedding licence. There were the two names in the sweet old visionary connexion, David Copperfield and Dora Spenlow; and there in the corner was that parental Institution the Stamp-office, looking down upon our union; and there, in the printed form of words, was the Archbishop of Canterbury invoking a blessing on us, and doing it as cheap as could possibly be expected!

I doubt whether two young birds could have known less about keeping house, than I and my pretty Dora did. We had a servant, of course. She kept house for us. We had an awful time of it with Mary Anne.

Her name was Paragon. Her nature was represented to us, when we engaged her, as being feebly expressed in her name. She had a written character, as large as a Proclamation; and, according to this document, could do everything of a domestic nature that ever I heard of, and a great many things that I never did hear of. She was a woman in the prime of life; of a severe countenance; and subject (particularly in the arms) to a sort of perpetual measles. She had a cousin in the Life Guards, with such long legs that he looked like the afternoon shadow of somebody else. She was warranted sober and honest. And I am therefore willing to believe that she was in a fit when we found her under the boiler; and that the deficient teaspoons were attributable to the dustman. She was the cause of our first little quarrel.

"My dearest life," I said one day to Dora, "do you think Mary Anne has any idea of time?"

"Why, Doady?" ~~inquired Dora, looking up from her drawing~~.

"My love, because it's five, and we were to have dined at four."

Dora glanced at the clock, and hinted that she thought it was too fast.

"On the contrary, my love, it's a few minutes too slow."

My little wife came and sat upon my knee, to coax me to be quiet, and drew a line with her pencil down the middle of my nose; but I couldn't dine off that, though it was very agreeable.

"Don't you think, my dear, it would be better for you to remonstrate with Mary Anne?"

"Oh no, please! I couldn't, Doady!"

"Why not, my love?"

"Oh, because I am such a little goose, and she knows I am!"

I thought this sentiment so incompatible with the establishment of any system of check on Mary Anne, that I frowned a little.

"Oh, what ugly wrinkles in my bad boy's forehead!" ~~said Dora, and still being~~ on my knee, She sat ~~she~~ traced them with her pencil; putting it to her rosy lips to make it mark blacker, and working

and

at my forehead with a quaint little mockery of being industrious, that quite delighted me in spite of myself.

"There's a good child," said Dora, "it makes its face so much prettier to laugh."

"But my love," said I.

"No, no! please!" cried Dora, with a kiss, "don't be a naughty Blue Beard! Don't be serious!"

"My precious wife," said I, "we must be serious sometimes. Come! Sit down on this chair, close beside me! Give me the pencil! There! Now let us talk sensibly. You know, dear;" what a little hand it was to hold, and what a tiny wedding-ring it was to see! "You know, my love, it is not exactly comfortable to have to go out without one's dinner. Now, is it?"

"N—n—no!" replied Dora, faintly.

"My love, how you tremble!"

"Because I KNOW you're going to scold me," exclaimed Dora, in a piteous voice.

"My sweet, I am only going to reason."

"Oh, but reasoning is worse than scolding! I didn't marry to be reasoned with. If you meant to reason with such a poor little thing as I am, you ought to have told me so, you cruel boy!"

I tried to pacify Dora, but she turned away her face, and shook her curls from side to side, and said, "You cruel, cruel boy!" so many times, that I really did not exactly know what to do. So I took a few turns up and down the room in my uncertainty, and came back again.

"Dora, my darling!"

"No, I am not your darling. Because you *must* be sorry that you married me, or else you wouldn't reason with me!" returned Dora.

I felt so injured by the inconsequential nature of this charge, that it gave me courage to be grave.

"Now, my own Dora, you are very childish, and are talking nonsense. You must remember, I am sure, that I was obliged to go out yesterday when dinner was half over; and that, the day before, I was made quite unwell by being obliged to eat underdone veal in a hurry; to-day, I don't dine at all—and I am afraid to say how long we waited for breakfast—and *then* the water didn't boil. I don't mean to reproach you, my dear, but this is not comfortable."

"Oh, you cruel, cruel boy, to say I am a disagreeable wife!"

"Now, my dear Dora, you must know that I never said that!"

"You said I wasn't comfortable!"

"I said the house-keeping was not comfortable."

"It's exactly the same thing! and I wonder, I do, at your making such ungrateful speeches. When you know that the other day, when you said you would like a little bit of fish, I went out myself, miles and miles, and ordered it, to surprise you."

"And it was very kind of you, my own darling, and I felt it so much that I wouldn't on any account have mentioned that you bought a salmon—which was too much for two. Or that it cost one pound six—which was more than we can afford."

"You enjoyed it very much," sobbed Dora. "And you said I was a mouse."

"And I'll say so again, my love, a thousand times!"

I said it a thousand times, and more, and went on saying it until Mary Anne's cousin deserted into our coal-hole, and was brought out, to our great amazement, by a piquet of his companions in arms, who took him away handcuffed, in a procession that covered our front-garden with disgrace. This nerved me to get rid of Mary Anne; and after an interval of Mrs. Kidgerbury—the oldest inhabitant of Kentish Town, who went out charing, but was too feeble to execute her conceptions of that art,—we found another treasure, who was one of the most amiable of women, but who generally made a point of falling either up or down the kitchen stairs with the tray. The ravages committed by this unfortunate, rendering her dismissal necessary, she was succeeded (with intervals of Mrs. Kidgerbury) by a long line of Incapables; terminating in a young person of genteel appearance, who went to Greenwich Fair in Dora's bonnet.

Everybody we had anything to do with, seemed to cheat us. Our appearance in a shop was a signal for the damaged goods to be brought out immediately. If we bought a lobster, it was full of water. All our meat turned out tough, and there was hardly any crust to our loaves. In search of the principle on which joints ought to be roasted, to be roasted enough and not too much, I myself referred to the Cookery-Book, and found it there established as the allowance of a quarter of an hour to every pound, and say a quarter over. But the principle always failed us.

As to the washerwoman pawning the clothes, and coming in a state of penitent intoxication to apologize, I suppose that might have happened several times to anybody. Also the chimney on fire, the parish engine, and perjury on the part of the Beadle. But I apprehend we were personally unfortunate in engaging a servant with a taste for cordials, who swelled our running account for porter at the public-house by such inexplicable items as "quartern rum shrub (Mrs. C.)" "Half-quartern gin and cloves (Mrs. C.)" "Glass rum and peppermint (Mrs. C.)"—the parenthesis always referring to Dora, who was supposed, it appeared on explanation, to have imbibed the whole of these refreshments.

Then, we kept a page. The principal function of this retainer was to quarrel with the cook; in which respect he was a perfect Whittington, without his cat, or the remotest chance of being made Lord Mayor. He lived in a hail of saucepan-lids. He would shriek for help on the most improper occasions—as when we had a little dinner or a few friends in the evening—and would come tumbling out of the kitchen, with iron missiles flying after him. We wanted to get rid of him, but he was very much attached to us, and wouldn't go, until one day he stole Dora's watch, and spent the produce (he was always a weak-minded boy) in incessantly riding up and down between London and Uxbridge outside the coach.

our whose

the Police Office

the Police Office

He was taken to Bow Street, as well as I remember, on the completion of his fifteenth journey; when four-and-sixpence, and a second-hand fife which he couldn't play, were found upon his person.

stet.

He was tried and ordered to be transported. Even then he couldn't be quiet, but was always writing us letters; and he wanted so much to see Dora before he went away, that Dora went to visit him, and fainted when she found herself inside the iron bars. I had no peace of my life until he was expatriated, and made (as I afterwards heard) a shepherd of, "up the country" somewhere; I have no geographical idea where.

"I am very sorry for all this, Doady," said Dora. "Will you call me a name I want you to call me?"

"What is it, my dear?"

"It's a stupid name—Child-wife. When you are going to be angry with me, say to yourself 'it's only my Child-wife.' When I am very disappointing, say, 'I knew, a long time ago, that she would make but a Child-wife.' When you miss what you would like me to be, and what I should like to be, and what I think I never can be, say, 'Still my foolish Child-wife loves me.' For indeed I do."

Her hands were clasped upon my shoulder, and her chin rested on them, and her eyes looked quietly into mine. I invoke the innocent figure that I dearly loved, to come out of the mists and shadows of the Past, and to turn its gentle head towards me once again, and to bear witness that it was made happy by what I answered.

VI

CHAPTER VI

I HEARD a footstep on the stairs one day. I knew it to be Mr. Peggotty's. It came nearer, nearer rushed into the room.

"Mas'r Davy, I've found her! I lay my dear child last night in my lodging here in Lunnon! I thank my Heavenly Father for having guided of me in His own ways to my darling!"

As he raised his sinewy hand to Heaven, I could not help observing what power and force of character it expressed.

"When my Em'ly found out as she was deceived, and when she took flight from the house in foreign parts wheer she was made a pris'ner by that theer spotted snake, she took flight in the night. It was a dark night, with a many stars a shining. She was wild. She ran along the sea beach,

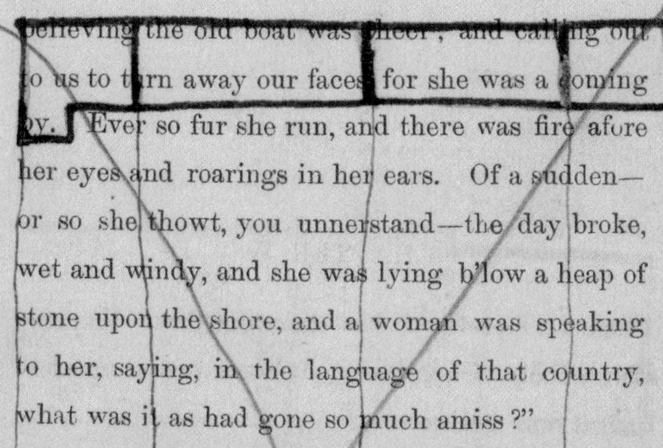

believing the old boat was cheer; and calling out to us to turn away our faces, for she was a coming by. Ever so fur she run, and there was fire afore her eyes and roarings in her ears. Of a sudden—or so she thowt, you unnerstand—the day broke, wet and windy, and she was lying b'low a heap of stone upon the shore, and a woman was speaking to her, saying, in the language of that country, what was it as had gone so much amiss?"

He saw everything he related. It passed before him, as he spoke, ~~vividly~~.

"As Em'ly's eyes—which was heavy—see this woman better, she know'd as she was one of them as she had often talked to on the beach. Fur, though she had run (as I have said) ever so fur in the night, she had oftentimes wandered long ways partly afoot, partly in boats and carriages, and know'd all that country, 'long the coast, miles and miles. She hadn't no children of her own, this woman, being a young wife; but she was a looking to have one afore long. And may my prayers go up to Heaven that 'twill be a happ'ness to her, and a comfort, and a honour, all her life! May it love her and be dootiful to her in her old age; helpful of her at the last; a Angel to her heer, and heerafter! Em'ly told her, and she took her home.

He was more affected by this act of kindness than I had ever seen him affected by anything since the night she went away.

"It was a little cottage, you may suppose, but she found space for Em'ly in it,—her husband was away at sea,—and she kep it secret, and prevailed upon such neighbours as she had (theer was not many near) to keep it secret too. Em'ly was took bad with fever, and what is very strange to me is,—maybe 'tis not so strange to scholars,—the language of that country went out of her head, and she could only speak her own, that no one understood. She recollects, as if she had dreamed it, that she lay there, always a talking her own tongue, always believing as the old boat was round the next pint in the bay, and begging and imploring of 'em to send theer and tell how

to her Theer.

fell into the weakness of the littlest child.

she was dying, and bring back a message of forgiveness, if it was on'y a wured. How long this lasted, I doen't know; but then there come a sleep; and in that sleep, from being a many times stronger than her own self, she fell into the weakness of the littlest child."

Here he stopped, as if for relief from the terrors of his own description.

"It was a pleasant arternoon when she awoke; and so quiet, that there warn't a sound but the rippling of that blue sea without a tide, upon the shore. It was her belief, at first, that she was at home upon a Sunday morning; but, the vine leaves as she see at the winder, and the hills beyond, warn't home, and contradicted of her. Then, come in her friend, to watch alongside of her bed; and then she know'd as the old boat warn't round that next pint in the bay no more but was fur off; and know'd where she was, and why; and broke out a crying on that good young woman's bosom!"

He could not speak of this good friend of

Emily's. It was in vain to try. He broke down again, endeavouring to bless her!

"That done my Em'ly good, and she begun to mend. But, the language of that country was quite gone from her, and she was forced to make signs. So she went on, getting better from day to day, slow, but sure, and trying to learn the names of common things—names as she seemed never to have heerd in all her life—till one evening come, when she was a setting at her window, looking at a little girl at play upon the beach. And of a sudden this child held out her hand, and said, what would be in English, 'Fisherman's daughter, here's a shell!'—for you are to unnerstand that they used at first to call her 'Pretty lady,' as the general way in that country is, and that she had taught 'em to call her 'Fisherman's daughter' instead. The child says of a sudden, 'Fisherman's daughter, here's a shell!' Then Em'ly unnerstands her; and she answers, bursting out a crying; and it all comes back!

she

"When ~~Em'ly~~ she got strong again, she cast about

She

to leave that good young creetur, and get to her own country. The husband was come home, then; and the two together put her aboard a small trader bound to Leghorn, and from that to France. She had a little money; but it was less than little as they would take for all they done. I'm a'most glad on it, though they was so poor! What they done is laid up wheer neither moth nor rust doth corrupt, and wheer thieves do not break through nor steal. Mas'r Davy, it'll outlast all the treasure in the wureld.

"Em'ly got to France, and took service to wait on travelling ladies at a inn in the port. Theer, theer come, one day, that snake.—Let him never come nigh me. I doen't know what hurt I might do him!—Soon as she see him, without him seeing her, all her fear and wildness returned upon her, and she fled afore the very breath he draw'd. She come to England, and was set ashore at Dover.

"I doen't know for sure, when her art begun to fail her; but all the way to England she had thowt to come right straight to her dear home.

All

Soon as she got to England she turned her face tow'rds it. But, fear of not being forgiv, fear of being pinted at, fear of some of us being dead along of her, fear of many things, turned her from it, kiender by force, upon the road. "Uncle, uncle,' she says to me last night, 'I turned back, when my heart was full of prayers that I might crawl to the old doorstep, in the night, kiss it, lay my wicked face upon it, and theer be found dead in the morning.'

'She come to London. She—as had never seen it in her life—alone—without a penny—young—so pretty—come to London. A'most the moment as she lighted heer, all so desolate, she found (as she believed) a friend, a decent woman as spoke to her about the needle-work as she had been brought up to do, about finding plenty of it fur her, about a lodging for the night, and making secret inquiration concerning of me and all at home to-morrow. When my child stood upon the brink of more than I can say or think on—I found and saved her!'

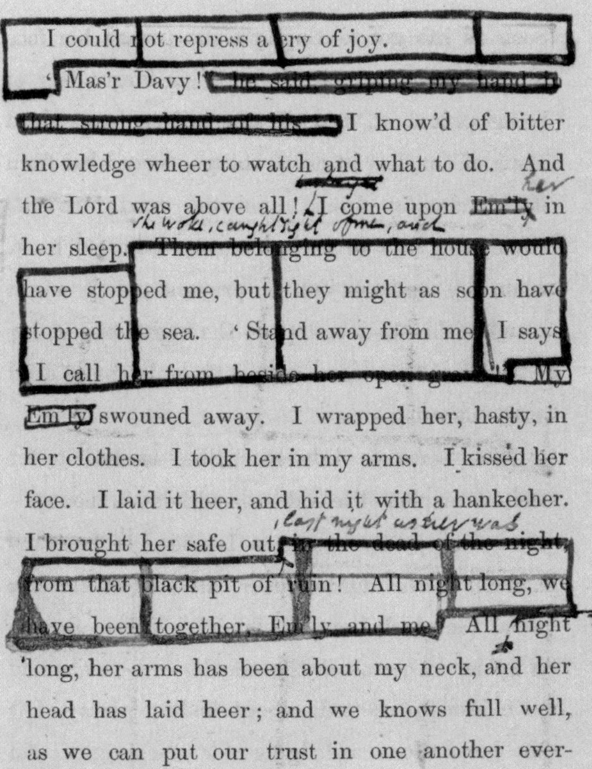

I could not repress a cry of joy.

'Mas'r Davy!' he said, gripping my hand in that strong hand of his, 'I know'd of bitter knowledge wheer to watch and what to do. And the Lord was above all! I come upon Em'ly in her sleep. Them belonging to the house would have stopped me, but they might as soon have stopped the sea. 'Stand away from me,' I says, 'I call her from beside her open grave!' My Em'ly swouned away. I wrapped her, hasty, in her clothes. I took her in my arms. I kissed her face. I laid it heer, and hid it with a hankecher. I brought her safe out, in the dead of the night, from that black pit of ruin! All night long, we have been together, Em'ly and me. All night long, her arms has been about my neck, and her head has laid heer; and we knows full well, as we can put our trust in one another evermore."

He ceased to speak, and his hand upon the table rested there in perfect repose, with a resolution in it that might have conquered lions.

her

She woke, caught sight of me, and

, last night as her was.

"You have made up your mind as to the future, good friend?"

"Yes, Mas'r Davy, theer's mighty countries, fur from heer. Our future life lays over the sea."

As he gave me both his hands, hurrying to return to the one charge of his noble existence, I thought of Ham. Who would break the intelligence to him? Mr. Peggotty thought of everything. He had already written to the poor fellow, and had the letter in the pocket of his rough coat, ready for the post. I asked him for it, and said I would go down to Yarmouth, and talk to Ham myself before I gave it him, and prepare him for its contents. He thanked me very earnestly, and we parted, with the understanding that I would go down by the Mail that same night. In the evening I started.

"Don't you think that," I asked the coachman, in the first stage out of London, "a very remarkable sky? I don't remember to have ever seen one like it."

"Nor I. That's wind, sir. There'll be mischief done at sea before long."

It was a murky confusion—here and there blotted with a colour like the colour of the smoke from damp fuel—of flying clouds tossed up into most remarkable heaps, suggesting greater heights in the clouds than there are depths below them to the bottom of the deepest hollows in the earth; through which the wild moon seemed to plunge headlong, as if, in a dread disturbance of the laws of nature, she had lost her way. There had been a wind all day; and it was rising then, with an extraordinary great sound. In another hour it had much increased, and the sky was more overcast, and it blew hard.

But, as the night advanced, the clouds closing in and densely overspreading the whole sky then very dark, it came on to blow, harder and harder. It still increased, until our horses could scarcely face the wind. Many times, in the dark part of the night (it was then late in September, when the nights were not short), the leaders turned about, or came to a dead stop; and we were often in serious apprehension that the coach would be blown over. Sweeping gusts of rain came up before this storm, like showers of steel; and at those times, when there was any shelter of trees or lee walls to be got, we were fain to stop, in a sheer impossibility of continuing the struggle.

When the day broke, the wind blew harder and harder. I had been in Yarmouth when the seamen said it blew great guns, but I had never known the like of this, or anything approaching to it. We came to Ipswich—very late, having had to fight every inch of ground since we were ten miles out of London; and found a cluster of people in the market-place, who had risen from their beds in the night, fearful of falling chimneys. Some of these told us of great sheets of lead having been ripped off a high church-tower, and flung into a bye-street. Others had to tell of country people, coming in from neighbouring villages, who had seen great trees lying torn out of the earth, and whole ricks scattered about the roads and fields. Still, there was no abatement in the storm, but it blew harder.

As we struggled on, nearer and nearer to the sea, from which this mighty wind was blowing dead on shore, its force became more and more terrific. When we came within sight of the sea, the waves on the horizon, seen at intervals above the rolling abyss, were like glimpses of another shore with towers and buildings. When at last we got into the town, the people came out to their doors, all aslant and with streaming hair, making a wonder of the mail that had come through such a night storm.

The tremendous sea itself, when I could find sufficient pause to look at it, in the agitation of the blinding wind, the flying stones and sand, and the awful noise, confounded me. As the high watery walls came rolling in, and tumbled into surf, they looked as if the least would engulf the town. As the receding wave swept back with a hoarse roar, it seemed to scoop out deep caves in

when I came to my journey's end,

when I came
to my
journey's end,

the beach. When some white-headed billows thundered on, and dashed themselves to pieces before they reached the land, every fragment of the late whole seemed possessed by the full might of its wrath, rushing to be gathered to the composition of another monster. Undulating hills were changed to valleys; undulating valleys were lifted up to hills; masses of water shivered and shook the beach with a booming sound; every shape rolled on, as soon as made, to change its shape and place, and beat another shape and place away; the ideal shore on the horizon with its towers and buildings, rose and fell; the clouds flew fast and thick; I seemed to see a rending and upheaving of all nature.

Not finding Ham among the people whom this memorable wind—for it is still remembered down there as the greatest ever known to blow upon that coast—had brought together on the beach, I made my way to his house. It was shut; and as no one answered to my knocking, I went by back ways and bye-lanes to the yard where he worked

, on a job of shipwright's work,

I learned ~~there~~ that he had gone some miles away, ~~to meet a sudden exigency of ship-repairing in which his skill was required;~~ but that he would be back to-morrow morning, in good time.

, on a job of shipwright's work,

So,

So, I went back to the inn; and when I had washed and dressed, and tried to sleep, but in vain, it was ~~five o'clock~~ late in the afternoon. I had not sat five minutes by the coffee-room fire, when the waiter coming to stir it, ~~as an excuse for talking~~ told me that two colliers had gone down, with all hands, a few miles off; and that some other ships had been seen labouring hard in the Roads, and trying, in great distress, to keep off shore. Mercy on them, and on all poor sailors, said he, if we had another night like the last!

late

I could not eat, I could not sit still, I could not continue stedfast to anything. Something within me, ~~faintly answering~~ to the storm without, ~~tossed up~~ the ~~depths of my memory,~~ wild running ~~with~~ of the thundering sea. My dinner went away almost untasted, and I tried to refresh myself with a glass or two of wine. In vain. I walked to and fro, tried to read an old gazetteer, listened to the awful noises: looked at faces, scenes, and figures in the fire. At length, the ~~steady~~ ticking of the undisturbed clock on the wall, tormented me to that degree that I resolved to go to bed.

in bed

For hours I lay ~~there~~ *in bed*, listening to the wind and water; imagining, now, that I heard shrieks out at sea; now, that I distinctly heard the firing of signal guns; now, the fall of houses in the town. At length, my restlessness attained to such a pitch, that I hurried on my clothes, and went down-stairs. In the large kitchen, all the inn servants and some other watchers were clustered together, ~~about a table purposely moved away from the great chimney.~~ One man, ~~referring to the topic they had been discussing,~~ asked me *when I went in among them* whether I thought the souls of the collier-crews who had gone down, were out in the storm?

when I went in among them

I remained ~~there~~ *with these people,* I dare say, two hours. Once, I opened the yard-gate, and looked into the empty street. The sand, the sea-weed, and the flakes of foam, were driving by, and I was obliged to call for assistance before I could shut the gate again, and make it fast against the wind.

There was a dark gloom in my lonely chamber, when I at length returned to it; but I was tired now, and, getting into bed again, fell off a tower and down a precipice into the depths of sleep. I dreamed of being engaged with two dear friends —but who they were I don't know—at the siege of some town in a roar of cannonading.

The thunder of the cannon was so loud and incessant, that I could not hear something I much desired to hear, until I made a great exertion and awoke. It was broad day—eight or nine o'clock; the storm was raging, in lieu of the batteries; and some one was knocking and calling at my door.

"What is the matter?"

"A wreck! Close by!"

"What wreck?"

"A schooner, from Spain or Portugal, laden

until
broad day
when I
was
aroused, at

by

with fruit and wine. Make haste, sir, if you want to see her! It's thought, down on the beach, she'll go to pieces every moment."

Quick

QUICK

I wrapped myself in my clothes as quickly as I could, and ran into the street. Numbers of people were there before me, all running in one direction, to the beach. I ran the same way, outstripping a good many, and soon came facing the wild sea. Every appearance it had before presented, bore the expression of being *swelled*; and the height to which the breakers rose, and bore one another down, and rolled in, in interminable hosts, was most appalling.

where

,where

When I got there,—

When I got there,—

In the difficulty of hearing anything but wind and waves, and in the crowd, and the unspeakable confusion, and my first breathless efforts to stand against the weather, I was so confused that I looked out to sea for the wreck, and saw nothing but the foaming heads of the great waves. A half-dressed boatman standing next me, pointed to the left. Then, O great Heaven, I saw it, close in upon us!

laid a hand upon my arm, and

laid a hand upon my arm, and

One mast was broken short off, six or eight feet from the deck, and lay over the side, entangled in a maze of sail and rigging; and all that ruin, as the ship rolled and beat—which she did without a moment's pause, and with a violence quite inconceivable—beat the side as if it would stave it in. Some efforts were being made, to cut this portion of the wreck away; for, as the ship, which was broadside on, turned towards us in her rolling, I plainly descried her people at work with axes—especially one active figure with long curling hair. But, a great cry, which was audible even above the wind and water, rose from the shore at this moment; the sea, sweeping over the rolling wreck, made a clean breach, and carried men, spars, casks, planks, bulwarks, heaps of such toys, into the boiling surge.

The second mast was yet standing, with the rags of a rent sail, and a wild confusion of broken cordage flapping to and fro. The ship had struck once, the same boatman hoarsely said in my ear, and then lifted in and struck again. I understood him to add that she was parting amidships, and I could readily suppose so, for the rolling and beating were too tremendous for any human work to suffer long. As he spoke, there was another great cry of pity from the beach. Four men arose with the wreck out of the deep, clinging to the rigging of the remaining mast; uppermost, the active figure with the curling hair.

There was a bell on board; and as the ship rolled and dashed, like a desperate creature driven mad, now showing us the whole sweep of her deck, as she turned on her beam-ends towards the shore, now nothing but her keel as she sprung wildly over and turned towards the sea, this bell rang; and its sound, the knell of those unhappy men, was borne towards us on the wind. Again we lost her, and again she rose. Two men were gone. The agony on shore increased. Men groaned, and clasped their hands; women shrieked, and turned away their faces. Some ran wildly up and down, crying for help.

of the four

of the four

where no help could be. I found myself one of these, frantically imploring a knot of sailors whom I knew, not to let those two lost creatures perish before our eyes.

They were making out to me, in an agitated way—I don't know how, for the little I could hear I was scarcely composed enough to understand—that the life-boat had been bravely manned an hour ago, and could do nothing; and that as no man would be so desperate as to attempt to wade off with a rope, and establish a communication with the shore, there was nothing left to try; when I noticed that some new sensation moved the people on the beach, and saw them part, and Ham come breaking through them to the front.

Instantly, I ran to him, I held him back with both arms; and implored the men with whom I had been speaking, not to listen to him, not to let him stir from off that sand!

Another cry arose on shore; and looking to the wreck, we saw the cruel sail, with blow on

Instantly,

for I divined that he meant to wade off with an axe rope.

blow, beat off the lower of the two men, and fly up in triumph round the active figure left alone upon the mast.

Against such a sight, and against such determination as that of the calmly desperate man who was already accustomed to lead half the people present, I might as hopefully have entreated the wind. "Mas'r Davy," he said, cheerily grasping me by both hands, "if my time is come, 'tis come. If 't a'nt, I'll bide it. Lord above bless you, and bless all! Mates, make me ready! I'm a going off!"

I was swept away to some distance, where the people around me made me stay; urging, as I confusedly perceived, that he was bent on going, with help or without, and that I should endanger the precautions for his safety by troubling those with whom they rested. I saw hurry on the beach, and men running with ropes from a capstan that was there, and penetrating into a circle of figures that hid him from me. Then, I saw him standing alone, in a seaman's frock and

Stet

trowsers: a rope in his hand~~, or slung to his wrist~~: another round his body: and several of the best men holding to the latter~~, which he laid out himself, slack upon the shore, at his feet~~.

The wreck~~, even to my unpractised eye~~, was breaking up. I saw that she was parting in the middle, and that the life of the solitary man upon the mast hung by a thread. ~~Still, he clung to it.~~ He had a singular red cap on,—not like a sailor's cap, but of a finer colour; and as the few ~~yielding~~ planks between him and destruction rolled and bulged, and as his ~~anticipative~~ death-knell rung, he was seen by all of us to wave ~~it~~. I saw him do it now, and thought I was going distracted, when his action brought an old remembrance to my mind of a once dear friend—*the* once dear friend—Steerforth.

his cap. I

Ham watched the sea, ~~with the silence of suspended breath behind him, and the storm before~~, until there was a great retiring wave; when he dashed in after it, and in a moment was buffeting with the water, rising with the hills, falling with the valleys, lost beneath the foam; then he was drawn again to land.

He was hurt. I saw blood on his face, from where I stood; but he took no thought of that. He seemed to give them some directions for leaving him more free—or so I judged from the motion of his arm—and was gone as before.

And now he made for the wreck, rising with the hills, falling with the valleys, lost beneath the foam; borne in towards the shore, borne on towards the ship. The distance was nothing, but the power of the sea and wind made the strife deadly. At length he neared the wreck. He was so near, that with one more of his vigorous strokes he would be clinging to it,—when, a high green vast hill-side of water, moving on shoreward, from beyond the ship, he seemed to leap up into it with a mighty bound—and the ship was gone!

Some eddying fragments I saw in the sea, as if a mere cask had been broken in. Consterna-

Low — Low

They drew him to my very feet—insensible—dead. He was carried to the nearest house; and every means of restoration were tried; but he had been beaten to death by the great wave, and his generous heart was stilled for ever.

Lower — Lower

As I sat beside the bed, when hope was abandoned and all was done, a fisherman, who had known me when Emily and I were children, and ever since, whispered my name at the door.

"Sir, will you come over yonder?"

The old remembrance that had been recalled to me, was in his look. I asked him:

"Has a body come ashore?"

"Yes."

"Do I know it?"

He answered nothing. But, he led me to the shore. And on that part of it where she and I had looked for shells, two children—on that part of it where some lighter fragments of the old boat, blown down last night, had been scattered by the wind—among the ruins of the home he had wronged—I saw him lying with his head upon his arm, as I had often seen him lie at school.

THE END OF THE READING.

LONDON PRINTED BY WILLIAM CLOWES AND SONS, STAMFORD STREET.

DAVID COPPERFIELD: A Reading

In all, six chapters

INTRODUCTION TO DAVID COPPERFIELD.

I HAD known the odd dwelling house inhabited by Mr. Peggotty very well in my childhood, and I am sure I could not have been more charmed with it, if it had been Aladdin's palace, roc's egg and all. It was an old black barge or boat, high and dry on Yarmouth Sands, with an iron funnel sticking out of it for a chimney. There was a delightful floor cut in the side, and it was roofed in, and there were little windows in it. It was beautifully clean and as tidy as possible. There wer some lockers and boxes, and there was a table, and there was a Dutch clock, and there was a chest of drawers, and there was a tea-tray with a painting or it, and the tray was kept from tumbling down, by a Bible; and the tray, if it *had* tumbled down, would have smashed a quantity of cups and saucers and a teapot that were grouped around the book. On the walls were coloured pictures of Abraham in red going to sacrifice Isaac in blue; and of Daniel in yellow being cast into a den of green lions. Mr. Peggotty, as honest a seafaring man as ever breathed, dealt in lobsters, crabs, and crawfish.

As in my childhood, so in these days when I was a young man, Mr. Peggotty's household consisted of HIS ORPHAN NEPHEW HAM PEGGOTTY, a young shipwright; HIS ADOPTED NIECE LITTLE EMILY, ONCE MY SMALL SWEETHEART, NOW A BEAUTIFUL YOUNG WOMAN; AND MRS. GUMMIDGE. All three had been maintained at Mr. Peggotty's sole charge for years and years; and Mrs. Gummidge was the widow of his partner in a boat, who had died poor. She was very grateful, but she certainly would have been more agreeable if she had not constantly complained as she sat in the most comfortable corner by the fireside, that she was "a lone lorn creetur and everythink went contrairy with her."

Towards this old boat, I walked one memorable night, with my former schoolfellow and present dear friend, Steerforth; Steerforth, half a dozen years older than I; brilliant, handsome, easy, winning; whom I admired with my whole heart; for whom I entertained the most romantic feelings of fidelity and friendship. He had come down with me from London, and had entered with the greatest ardour into my scheme of visiting the old simple place and the old simple people.

There was no moon; and as he and I walked on the dark wintry sands towards the old boat, the wind sighed mournfully.

"This is a wild place, Steerforth, is it not?"

"Dismal enough in the dark, and the sea has a cry in it, as if it were hungry for us. Is that the boat, where I see a light yonder?"

"That's the boat."

We said no more as we approached the light, but made softly for the door. I laid my hand upon the latch; and whispering Steerforth to keep close to me, went in.

I was in the midst of the astonished family, whom I had not seen from my childhood, face to face with Mr. Peggotty, and holding out my hand to him, when Ham shouted:

"Mas'r Davy! It's Mas'r Davy!"

In a moment we were all shaking hands with one another, and asking one another how we did, and telling one another how glad we were to meet, and all talking at once. Mr. Peggotty was so overjoyed to see me, and to see my friend, that he did not know what to say or do, but kept over and over again shaking hands with me, and then with Steerforth, and then with me, and then ruffling his shaggy hair all over his head, and then laughing with such glee and triumph, that it was a treat to see him.

"Why, that you two gentl'men—gentl'men growed—should come to this here roof to-night, of all nights in my life, is such a merry-go-rounder as never happened afore, I do rightly believe! Em'ly, my darling, come here! Come here, my little witch! Theer's Mas'r Davy's friend; my dear! Theer's the gentl'man as you've heerd on, Em'ly. He comes to see you, along with Mas'r Davy, on the brightest night of your uncle's life as ever was or will be, horroar for it!"

Then he let her go; and as she ran into her little chamber looked round upon us, quite hot and out of breath with his uncommon satisfaction.

"If you two gentl'men—gentl'men growed now, and such gentl'men — don't ex-cuse me for being in a state of mind, when you understand matters, I'll arks your pardon. Em'ly, my dear!—She knows I'm a going to tell, and has made off.

LOW

"This here little Em'ly, sir," to Steerforth, "—her as you see a blushing here just now—

"This here little Em'ly of ours, has been, in our house, sir, what I suppose (I'm a ignorant man, but that's my belief) no one but a little bright-eyed creetur *can* be in a house. She ain't my child; I never had one; but I couldn't love her more, if she was fifty times my child. You understand! I couldn't do it!"

"I quite understand."

"I know you do, sir, and thankee well sir.

"There was a certain person as had know'd our Em'ly, from the time when her father was drownded; as had seen her constant; when a babby, when a young gal, when a woman. Not much of a person to look at, he warn't—something o' my own build—rough—a good deal o' the sou'-wester in him—wery salt—but, on the whole, a honest sort of a chap too, with his art in the right place."

I had never seen Ham grin to anything like the extent to which he sat grinning at us now.

"What does this here blessed tarpaulin go and do, but he loses that there art of his to our little Em'ly. He follers her about, he makes hisself a sort o' servant to her, he loses in a great measure his relish for his wittles, and in the long run he makes it clear to me wot's amiss.

"Well! I counsels him to speak to Em'ly. He's big enough, but he's bashfuller than a little un, and he says to me he doen't like. So *I* speak. 'What! *Him*!' says Em'ly. '*Him* that I've know'd so intimate so many year, and like so much! Oh, Uncle! I never can have *him*. He's such a good fellow!' I gives her a kiss, and I says no more to her than 'My dear, you're right to speak out, you're to choose for yourself, you're as free as a little bird.' Then I aways to him, and I says, 'I wish it could have been so, but it can't. But you can both be as you was, and wot I say to you is, Be as you was with her, like a man.' He says to me, a shaking of my hand, 'I will.!' he says. And he was—honourable, trew, and manful—going on for two year.

"All of a sudden, one evening—as it might be to-night—comes little Em'ly from her work, and him with her! There ain't so much in *that,* you'll say. No, sure, because he takes care on her, like a brother, arter dark, and indeed afore dark, and at all times. But this heer tarpaulin chap, he takes hold of her hand, and he cries out to me, joyful, 'Lookee here! This is to be my little wife!' And she says, half bold and half shy, and half a laughing and half a crying, 'Yes, uncle! If you please.'—If I please! Lord, as if I should do anythink else!—'If you please,' she says, 'I am steadier now, and I have thought better of it, and I'll be as good a little wife as I can to him, for he's a dear good fellow!' Then Missis Gummidge, she claps her hands like a play, and you come in. There! The murder's out! You come in! It took place this here present hour; and here's the man as'll marry her, the minute she's out of her time at the needlework."

Ham staggered, as well he might, under the blow Mr. Peggotty dealt him, as a mark of confidence and friendship; but feeling called upon to say something to us, he stammered:

"She warn't no higher than you was, Mas'r Davy—when you first come heer—when I thought what she'd grow up to be. I see her grow up—gentl'men—like a flower. I'd lay down my life for her—Mas'r Davy—Oh! most content and cheerful! There ain't a gentl'man in all the land—nor yet a sailing upon all the sea—that can love his lady more than I love her, though there's many a common man—as could say better—what he meant."

I thought it affecting to see such a sturdy fellow trembling in the strength of what he felt for the pretty little creature who had won his heart. I thought the simple confidence reposed in us by Mr. Peggotty and by himself, was touching. I was affected by the story altogether. I was filled with pleasure; but at first, with an indescribably sensitive pleasure, that a very little would have changed to pain.

Therefore, if it had depended upon me to touch the prevailing chord among them with any skill, I should have made a poor hand of it. But it depended upon Steerforth; and he did it with such address, that in a few minutes we were all as easy as possible.

"Mr. Peggotty," he said, "you are a thoroughly good fellow, and deserve to be as happy as you are to-night. My hand upon it! Ham, I give you joy, my boy. My hand upon that, too! Davy, stir the fire, and make it a brisk one! And Mr. Peggotty, unless you can induce your gentle niece to come back, I shall go. Any

gap at your fireside on such a night—such a gap least of all—I wouldn't make, for the wealth of the Indies!"

So, Mr. Peggotty went to fetch little Em'ly. At first little Em'ly didn't like to come, and then Ham went. Presently they brought her to the fireside, very much confused, and very shy,—but she soon became more assured when she found how Steerforth spoke to her; how skilfully he avoided anything that would embarrass her; how he talked to Mr. Peggotty of boats, and ships, and tides, and fish; how delighted he was with that boat and all belonging to it; how lightly and easily he carried on, until he brought us, by degrees, into a charmed circle.

But he set up no monopoly of the conversation. He was silent and attentive when little Emily talked across the fire to me of our old childish wanderings upon the beach, to pick up shells and pebbles; he was very silent and attentive when I asked her if she recollected how I used to love her, and how we used to walk about that dim old flat, hours and hours, and how the days sported by us as if Time himself had not grown up then, but were a child like ourselves, and always at play. She sat all the evening, in her old little corner by the fire—Ham beside her. I could not satisfy myself whether it was in her little tormenting way, or in a maidenly reserve before us, that she kept quite close to the wall, and away from Ham; but I observed that she did so, all the evening.

As I remember, it was almost midnight when we took our leave. We had had some biscuit and dried fish for supper, and Steerforth had produced from his pocket a flask of Hollands. We parted merrily; and as they all stood crowded round the door to light us on our road, I saw the sweet blue eyes of little Em'ly peeping after us, from behind Ham, and heard her soft voice calling to us to be careful how we went.

"A most engaging little Beauty!" said Steerforth, taking my arm. "Well! It's a quaint place, and they are quaint company; and it's quite a new sensation to mix with them."

"How fortunate we are, too, Steerforth, to have arrived to witness their happiness in that intended marriage! I never saw people so happy. How delightful to see it!"

"Yes—that's rather a chuckle-headed fellow for the girl. Isn't he?"

I felt a shock in this cold reply. But turning quickly upon him, and seeing a laugh in his eyes, I answered:

"Ah, Steerforth! It's well for you to joke about the poor! But when I see how perfectly you understand them, and how you can enter into happiness like this plain fisherman's, I know there is not a joy, or sorrow, or any emotion, of such people, that can be indifferent to you. And I admire and love you for it, Steerforth, twenty times the more!"

To my surprise, he suddenly said, with nothing, that I could see, to lead to it:

"Daisy, I wish to God I had had a judicious father these last twenty years!

"You know my mother has always doted on me and spoilt me. I wish with all my soul I had been better guided! I wish with all my soul, I could guide myself better!"

There was a passionate dejection in his manner that quite amazed me. He was more unlike himself than I could have supposed possible.

"It would be better to be this poor Peggotty, or his lout of a nephew, than be myself, twenty times richer and twenty times wiser, and be the torment to myself that I have been in that Devil's bark of a boat within the last half-hour."

I was so confounded by the change in him that at first I could only regard him in silence as he walked at my side. At length I asked him, to tell me what had happened to cross him so unusually.

"Tut, it's nothing—nothing, Davy! I must have had a nightmare, I think. What old women call the horrors, have been creeping over me from head to foot. I have been afraid of myself."

"You are afraid of nothing else, I think."

"Perhaps not, and yet may have enough to be afraid of, too. Well! so it goes by! Daisy—for though that's not the name your godfathers and godmothers gave you, you're such a fresh fellow that it's the name I best like to call you by—and I wish, I wish, I wish, you could give it to me!"

"Why, so I can, if I choose."

"Daisy, if anything should ever happen to separate us, you must think of me at my best, old boy. Come! let us make that bargain. Think of me at my best, if circumstances should ever part us!"

"You have no best to me, Steerforth, and no worst. You are always equally loved and cherished in my heart."

I was up, to go away alone, next morning with the dawn, and, having dressed as quietly as I could, looked into his room. He was fast asleep; lying, easily, with his head upon his arm, as I had often seen him lie at school.

The time came in its season, and that was very soon, when I almost wondered that nothing troubled his repose, as I looked at him then. But he slept—let me think of him so again—as I had often seen him sleep at school; and thus, in this silent hour I left him.

—Never more, O God forgive you, Steerforth! to touch that passive hand in love and friendship. Never, never, more!

DAVID COPPERFIELD.

CHAPTER THE SECOND

Some months elapsed before I again found myself down in that part of the country, and approaching the old boat by night.

It was a dark evening, and rain was beginning to fall, when I came within sight of Mr. Peggotty's house, and of the light within it shining through the window. A little floundering across the sand, which was heavy, brought me to the door, and I went in. I was bidden to a little supper; Emily was to be married to Ham that day fortnight, and this was the last time I was to see her in her maiden life.

It looked very comfortable, indeed. Mr. Peggotty had smoked his evening pipe, and there were preparations for supper by-and-by. The fire was bright, the ashes were thrown up, the locker was ready for little Emily in her old place. In her own old place sat my dear old nurse, Mr. Peggotty's sister. Mrs. Gummidge appeared to be fretting a little, in her own corner; and consequently looked quite natural.

"You're first of the lot, Mas'r Davy! Sit ye down, sir. It ain't o' no use saying welcome to you, but you're welcome, kind and hearty."

Here Mrs. Gummidge groaned.

"Cheer up, cheer up, Mrs. Gummidge!" said Mr. Peggotty.

"No, no, Dan'l! It ain't o' no use telling me to cheer up, when everythink goes contrairy with me. "Nothink's nat'ral to me but to be lone and lorn."

After looking at Mrs. Gummidge for some moments, with great sympathy,

Mr. Peggotty glanced at the Dutch clock, rose, snuffed the candle, and put it in the window.

"Theer! Theer we are, Missis Gummidge!" Mrs. Gummidge slightly groaned again. "Theer we are, Mrs. Gummidge. Lighted up, accordin' to custom! You're a wondering' what that's fur, sir! Well, it's fur our little Em'ly. You see, the path ain't over light or cheerful arter dark; and when I'm here at the hour as she's a comin' home from her needlework down-town, I puts the light in the winder. That, you see, meets two objects. She says to herself, says Em'ly, 'Theer's home!' she says. And likeways, says Em'ly, 'My uncle's theer!' Fur if I ain't theer, I never have no light showed."

"You may say this is like a Babby Sir.

"Well, I doen't know but what I am a babby in regard o' Em'ly. Not to look at, but to—to consider on, you know. *I* doen't care, bless you! Now I tell you. When I go a looking and looking about that theer pritty house of our Em'ly's, all got ready for her to be married, if I doen't feel as if the littlest things was her, a'most. I takes 'em up, and I puts 'em down, and I touches of 'em as delicate as if they was our Em'ly. So 't is with her little bonnets and that. I couldn't see one on 'em rough used a purpose—not fur the whole wureld.

"It's my opinion, you see, as this is along of my havin' played with Em'ly so much when she was a child, and havin' made believe as we was Turks, and French, and sharks, and every wariety of forinners—bless you, yes; and lions and whales, and I don't know what all!—when she warn't no higher than my knee. I've got into the way on it, you know. Why, this here candle, now! *I* know wery well that arter she's married and gone, I shall put that candle theer, just the same as now, and sit afore the fire, pretending I'm expecting of her, like as I'm a doing now. Why, at the present minute, when I see the candle sparkle up, I says to myself, 'She's a looking at it! Em'ly's a coming!' Right too! fur here she is!"

No: it was only Ham. The night should have turned more wet since I came in, for he had a large sou'wester hat on, slouched over his face.

"Where's Em'ly?"

Ham made a movement as if she were outside. Mr. Peggotty took the light from the window, trimmed it, put it on the table, and was stirring the fire, when Ham, who had not moved, said:

"Mas'r Davy, will you come out a minute, and see what Em'ly and me has got to show you?"

As I passed him, I saw, to my astonishment and fright, that he was deadly pale. He closed the door upon us. Only upon us two.

"Ham! What's the matter?"

"My love, Mas'r Davy—the pride and hope of my art—her that I'd have died for, and would die for now—she's gone!"

"Gone?"

"Em'ly's run away!

"You're a scholar, and know what's right and best. What am I to say, in-doors? How am I ever to break it to him, Mas'r Davy?"

I saw the door move, and tried to hold the latch, to gain a moment's time. It was too late. Mr. Peggotty thrust forth his face; and never could I forget the change that came upon it when he saw us, if I were to live five hundred years.

I remember a great wail and cry, and the women hanging about him, and we all standing in the room; I with an open letter in my hand, which Ham had given me; Mr. Peggotty, with his vest torn open, his hair wild, his face and lips white, and blood trickling down his bosom (it had sprung from his mouth, I think).

"Read it, sir; slow, please. I doen't know as I can understand."

In the midst of the silence of death, I read thus, from the blotted letter Ham had given me. In Emily's hand—addressed to himself.

" 'When you, who love me so much better than I ever have deserved, even when my mind was innocent, see this, I shall be far away.'

" 'When I leave my dear home—my dear home—oh, my dear home!—in the morning,' "

—the letter bore date on the previous night:

" '—It will be never to come back, unless he brings me back a lady. This will be found at night, many hours after, instead of me. For mercy's sake, tell uncle that I never loved him half so dear as now. Oh, don't remember you and I were ever to be married—but try to think as if I died when I was little, and was buried somewhere. Pray Heaven that I am going away from, have compassion on my uncle! Be his comfort. Love some good girl, that will be what I was once to uncle, and that will be true to you, and worthy of you, and know no shame but me. God bless all! If he don't bring me back a lady, and I don't pray for my own self, I'll pray for all. My parting love to uncle. My last tears, and my last thanks, for uncle!' "

That was all.

He stood, long after I had ceased to read, still looking at me.

Slowly, at last, he moved his eyes from my face, and cast them round the room.

"Who's the man? I want to know his name."

Ham glanced at me, and suddenly I felt a shock.

"Mas'r Davy! Go out a bit, and let me tell him what I must. You doen't ought to hear it, sir."

I sank down in a chair, and tried to utter some reply; but my tongue was fettered, and my sight was weak. For I felt that the man was my friend—the friend I had unhappily introduced there—Steerforth, my old schoolfellow and my friend.

"I want to know his name!"

"Mas'r Davy's frend. He's the man."

"Mas'r Davy, it ain't no fault of yourn—and I am far from laying of it to you—but it is your friend Steerforth, and he's a damned villain!"

Mr. Peggotty moved no more, until he seemed to wake all at once, and pulled down his rough coat from its peg in a corner.

"Bear a hand with this! I'm struck of a heap, and can't do it. Bear a hand, and help me. Well! Now give me that theer hat!"

Ham asked him whither he was going?

"I'm a going to seek my niece. I'm a going to seek my Em'ly. I'm a going, first, to stave in that theer boat as he gave me, and sink it where I would have drownded *him*, as I'm a livin' soul, if I had had one thought of what was in him! As he sat afore me, in that boat, face to face, strike me down dead, but I'd have drownded him, and thought it right!—I'm a going fur to seek my niece."

"Where?"

"Anywhere! I'm a going to seek my niece through the wureld. I'm a going to find my poor niece in her shame, and bring her back wi' my comfort and forgiveness. No one stop me! I tell you I'm a going to seek my niece! I'm a going to seek her fur and wide!"

Mrs. Gummidge, came between them, in a fit of crying. "No, no, Dan'l, not as you are now. Seek her in a little while, my lone lorn Dan'l, and that'll be but right; but not as you are now. Sit ye down, and give me your forgiveness for having ever been a worrit to you, Dan'l—what have *my* contrairies ever been to

this!—and let us speak a word about them times when she was first a orphan, and when Ham was too, and when I was a poor widder woman, and you took me in. It'll soften your poor heart, Dan'l, and you'll bear your sorrow better; for you know the promise, Dan'l, 'As you have done it unto one of the least of these, you have done it unto me;' and that can never fail under this roof, that's been our shelter for so many, many year!"

He was quite passive now; and when I heard him crying, the impulse that had been upon me to go down upon my knees, and curse Steerforth, yielded to a better feeling. My overcharged heart found the same relief as his, and I cried too.

CHAPTER III

AT this period of my life I lived in my top set of chambers in Buckingham Street, Strand, London, and was over head and ears in love with Dora. I lived principally on Dora and coffee. My appetite languished and I was glad of it, for I felt as though it would have been an act of perfidy towards Dora to have a natural relish for my dinner. I bought four sumptuous waistcoats—not for myself; *I* had no pride in them—for Dora. I took to wearing straw-coloured kid gloves in the streets. I laid the foundations of all the corns I have ever had. If the boots I wore at that period could only be produced and compared with the natural size of my feet, they would show in a most affecting manner what the state of my heart was.

Mrs. Crupp, the housekeeper of my chambers, must have been a woman of penetration; for, when this attachment was but a few weeks old, she found it out. She came up to me one evening when I was very low, to ask (she being afflicted with spasms) if I could oblige her with a little tincture of cardamums, mixed with rhubarb and flavoured with seven drops of the essence of cloves—or, if I had not such a thing by me—with a little brandy. As I had never even heard of the first remedy, and always had the second in the closet, I gave Mrs. Crupp a glass of the second; which (that I might have no suspicion of its being devoted to any improper use) she began to take immediately.

"Cheer up, sir," said Mrs. Crupp. "Excuse me. I know what it is, sir. There's a lady in the case."

"Mrs. Crupp?"

"Oh, bless you! Keep a good heart, sir? Never say die, sir! If she don't smile upon you, there's a many as will. You're a young gentleman to *be* smiled on, Mr. Copperfull, and you must learn your walue, sir."

Mrs. Crupp always called me Mr. Copperfull: firstly, no doubt, because it was not my name; and secondly, I am inclined to think, in some indistinct association with a washing-day.

"What makes you suppose there is any young lady in the case, Mrs. Crupp?"

"Mr. Copperfull, 'I'm a mother myself. Your boots and your waist is equally very small, and you don't eat enough, sir, nor yet drink.

"Sir, I've laundressed other young gentlemen besides you.

"It was but the gentleman which died here before yourself, that fell in love—with a barmaid—and had his waistcoats took in directly, though much swelled by drinking."

"Mrs. Crupp, I must beg you not to connect the young lady in my case with a barmaid, or anything of that sort, if you please."

"Mr. Copperfull, I'm a mother myself, and not likely. I ask your pardon, sir, if I intrude. I should never wish to intrude where I were not welcome. But you are a young gentleman, Mr. Copperfull, and my adwice to you is, to cheer up, sir, to keep a good heart, and to know your own walue. If you was to take to something, sir; if you was to take to skittles, now, which is healthy, you might find it divert your mind, and do you good."

I turned it off and changed the subject by informing Mrs. Crupp that I wished to entertain at dinner next day, my esteemed friends Traddles, and Mr. and Mrs. Micawber. And I took the liberty of suggesting a pair of soles, a small leg of mutton, and a pigeon pie. Mrs. Crupp broke out into rebellion on my first bashful hint in reference to her cooking the fish and joint. But, in the end, a compromise was effected; and Mrs. Crupp consented to achieve this feat, on condition that I dined from home for a fortnight afterwards.

A "young gal" whom I had previously employed on the motion of Mrs. Crupp was re-engaged, but on the stipulation that she only bring in the dishes, and then withdraw to the landing place, beyond the outer door, where a habit of sniffing she had contracted would be lost upon the guests.

Having laid in the materials for a bowl of punch, to be compounded by Mr. Micawber; having provided a bottle of lavender-water, two wax candles, a paper of mixed pins, and a pin-cushion, to assist Mrs. Micawber in her toilette, at my dressing-table; having also caused the fire in my bed-room to be lighted for Mrs. Micawber's convenience; and having laid the cloth with my own hands; I awaited the result with composure.

At the appointed time, my three visitors arrived together. Mr. Micawber with more shirt-collar than usual, and a new ribbon to his eye-glass; Mrs. Micawber with her cap in a parcel; Traddles carrying the parcel, and supporting Mrs. Micawber on his arm. They were all delighted with my residence. When I conducted Mrs. Micawber to my dressing-table, and she saw the scale on which it was prepared for her, she was in such raptures, that she called Mr. Micawber to come in and look.

"My dear Copperfield," said Mr. Micawber, "this is luxurious. This is a way of life which reminds me of the period when I was myself in a state of celibacy. I am at present established on what may be designated as a small and unassuming scale; but, you are aware that I have, in the course of my career, surmounted difficulties, and conquered obstacles. You are no stranger to the fact, that there have been periods of my life, when it has been requisite that I should pause, until certain expected events should turn up —when it has been necessary that I should fall back, before making what I trust I shall not be accused of presumption in terming—a spring. The present is one of those momentous stages in the life of man. You find me, fallen back, *for* a spring; and I have every reason to believe that a vigorous leap will shortly be the result."

I informed Mr. Micawber that I relied upon him for a bowl of punch, and led him to the lemons. I never saw a man so thoroughly enjoy himself as he stirred, and mixed, and tasted, and looked as if he were making, not mere punch, but a fortune for his family down to the latest posterity. As to Mrs. Micawber, I don't know whether it was the effect of the cap, or the lavender-water, or the pins, or the fire, or the wax-candles, but she came out of my room, comparatively speaking, lovely.

I suppose—I never ventured to inquire, but I suppose—that Mrs. Crupp, after frying the soles, was taken ill. Because we broke down at that point. The leg of mutton came up, very red inside, and very pale outside; besides having a foreign substance of a gritty nature sprinkled over it, as if it had had a fall into ashes. But we were not in a condition to judge of this fact from the appearance of the gravy, forasmuch as it had been all dropped on the stairs. The pigeon-pie was not bad, but it was a delusive pie: the crust being like a disappointing phrenological head: full of lumps and bumps, with nothing particular underneath. In short, the banquet was such a failure that I should have been quite unhappy—about the failure, I mean, for I was always unhappy about Dora—if I had not been relieved by the great good-humour of my company.

"My dear friend Copperfield," said Mr. Micawber, "accidents will occur in the best-regulated families; and especially in families not regulated by that pervading influence which sanctifies while it enhances the—a—I would say, in short, by the influence of Woman in the lofty character of Wife. If you will allow me to take the liberty of remarking that there are few comestibles better, in their way, than a Devil, and that I believe, with a little division of labour, we could accomplish a good one if the young person in attendance could produce a gridiron, I would put it to you, that this little misfortune may be easily repaired."

There was a gridiron in the pantry, on which my morning rasher of bacon was cooked. We had it out, in a twinkling; Traddles cut the mutton into slices; Mr. Micawber covered them with pepper, mustard, salt, and cayenne; I put them on the gridiron, turned them with a fork, and took them off, under Mr. Micawber's direction; and Mrs. Micawber heated some mushroom ketchup in a little saucepan. Under these circumstances, my appetite came back miraculously. I am ashamed to confess it, but I really believe I forgot Dora for a little while.

"Punch, my dear Copperfield," said Mr. Micawber, tasting it as soon as dinner

Tasting

was done, "like time and tide, waits for no man. Ah! it is at the present moment in high flavour. My love, will you give me your opinion?"

Mrs. Micawber pronounced it excellent.

"As we are quite confidential here, Mr. Copperfield," said Mrs. Micawber sipping

Sipping

her punch, "(Mr. Traddles being a part of our domesticity), I should much like to have your opinion on Mr. Micawber's prospects. I have consulted branches of my family on the course most expedient for Mr. Micawber to take, and it was, that he should immediately turn his attention to coals."

"To what, ma'am?"

"To coals. To the coal trade. Mr. Micawber was induced to think, on inquiry, that there might be an opening for a man of his talent in the Medway Coal Trade. Then, as Mr. Micawber very properly said, the first step to be taken clearly was, to go and *see* the Medway. Which we went and saw. I say 'we,' Mr. Copperfield; for I never will desert Mr. Micawber. I am a wife and mother, and I never will desert Mr. Micawber."

Traddles and I murmured our admiration.

"That," said Mrs. Micawber, "that, at least, is *my* view, my dear Mr. Copperfield and Mr. Traddles, of the obligation which I took upon myself when I repeated the irrevocable words 'I Emma, take thee, Wilkins.' I read the service over with a flat-candle, on the previous night, and the conclusion I derived from it was that I never could or would desert Mr. Micawber."

"My dear," said Mr. Micawber, a little impatiently, "I am not conscious that you are expected to do anything of the sort."

"We went," repeated Mrs. Micawber, "and saw the Medway. My opinion of the coal trade on that river, was, that it might require talent, but that it certainly requires capital. Talent, Mr. Micawber has; capital, Mr. Micawber has not. We saw, I think, the greater part of the Medway; and that was my individual conclusion. My family were then of opinion that Mr. Micawber should turn his attention to corn—on commission. But corn, as I have repeatedly said to Mr. Micawber, may be gentlemanly, but it is not remunerative. Commission to the extent of two and ninepence in a fortnight cannot, however limited our ideas, be considered remunerative."

We were all agreed upon that.

"Then," said Mrs. Micawber, who prided herself on taking a clear view of things, and keeping Mr. Micawber straight by her woman's wisdom, when he might otherwise go a little crooked, "then I naturally look round the world, and say, 'What is there in which a person of Mr. Micawber's talent is likely to succeed?'

"I may have a conviction that Mr. Micawber's manners peculiarly qualify him for the Banking business. I may argue within myself, that if *I* had a deposit at a banking-house, the manners of Mr. Micawber, as representing that banking-house, would inspire confidence, and extend the connexion. But if the various banking-houses refuse to avail themselves of Mr. Micawber's abilities, or receive the offer of them with contumely, what is the use of dwelling upon *that* idea? None. As to originating a banking-business, I may know that there are members of my family who, if they chose to place their money in Mr. Micawber's hands, might found an establishment of that description. But if they do *not* choose to place their money in Mr. Micawber's hands—which they don't—what is the use of that? Again I contend that we are no farther advanced than we were before."

I shook my head, and said, "Not a bit." Traddles also shook his head, and said, "Not a bit."

"What do I deduce from this?" Mrs. Micawber went on to say, still with the same air of putting a case lucidly. "What is the conclusion, my dear Mr. Copperfield, to which I am irresistibly brought? Am I wrong in saying, it is clear that we must live?"

I answered, "Not at all!" and Traddles answered, "Not at all!" and I found myself afterwards sagely adding, alone, that a person must either live or die.

"Just so," returned Mrs. Micawber. "It is precisely that.

"And here is Mr. Micawber without any suitable position or employment. Where does that responsibility rest? Clearly on society. Then I would make a fact so disgraceful known, and boldly challenge society to set it right. It appears to me, my dear Mr. Copperfield, that what Mr. Micawber has to do is to throw down the gauntlet to society, and say, in effect, 'Show me who will take that up. Let the party immediately step forward.'

"It appears to me, that what Mr. Micawber has to do, is to advertise in all the papers; to describe himself plainly as so and so, with such and such qualifications, and to put it thus: '*Now* employ me, on remunerative terms, and address, post paid, to *W. M.*, Post Office, Camden Town.' "

"For this purpose, I think Mr. Micawber ought to raise a certain sum of money—on a bill.

"If no member of my family, is possessed of sufficient natural feeling to negotiate that bill, then, my opinion is, that Mr. Micawber should go into the

City, should take that bill into the Money Market, and should dispose of it for what he can get."

I felt, but I am sure I don't know why, that this was highly self-denying and devoted in Mrs. Micawber, and I uttered a murmur to that effect. Traddles, who took his tone from me, did likewise, and really I felt that she was a noble woman—the sort of woman who might have been a Roman matron, and done all manner of troublesome heroic public actions.

I congratulated Mr. Micawber on the treasure he possessed. So did Traddles. Mr. Micawber extended his hand to each of us in succession, and then covered his face with his pocket-handkerchief—which I think had more snuff upon it than he was aware of. He then made tea for us in a most agreeable manner; and after tea we discussed a variety of topics before the fire; and she was good enough to sing us (in a small, thin, flat voice, which I remembered to have considered, when I first knew her, the very table-beer of acoustics) the favourite ballads of "The Dashing White Sergeant," and "Little Tafflin." For both of these songs Mrs. Micawber had been famous when she lived at home with her papa and mamma. Mr. Micawber told us, that when he heard her sing the first one, on the first occasion of his seeing her beneath the parental roof, she had attracted his attention in an extraordinary degree; but that when it came to Little Tafflin, he had resolved to win that woman or perish in the attempt.

It was between ten and eleven o'clock when Mrs. Micawber rose to replace her cap in the parcel, and to put on her bonnet. Mr. Micawber took the opportunity to slip a letter into my hand, with a whispered request that I would read it at my leisure. I also took the opportunity of my holding a candle over the bannisters to light them down, when Mr. Micawber was going first, leading Mrs. Micawber, to detain Traddles for a moment on the top of the stairs.

"Traddles, Mr. Micawber don't mean any harm; but, if I were you, I wouldn't lend him anything."

"My dear Copperfield, I haven't got anything to lend."

"You have got a name, you know."

"Oh! You call *that* something to lend?"

"Certainly."

"Oh! Yes, to be sure! I am very much obliged to you, Copperfield, but—I am afraid I have lent him that already."

"For the bill that is to go into the money market?"

"No. Not for that one. This is the first I have heard of that one. I have been thinking that he will most likely propose that one, on the way home. Mine's another."

"I hope there will be nothing wrong about it."

"I hope not. I should think not, though, because he told me, only the other day, that it was provided for. That was Mr. Micawber's expression, 'Provided for.'"

Mr. Micawber looking up at this juncture, I had only time to repeat my caution. Traddles thanked me, and descended. But I was much afraid, when I observed the good-natured manner in which he went down with Mrs. Micawber's cap in his hand, that he would be carried into the Money Market, neck and heels.

I returned to my fireside, and read Mr. Micawber's letter which was dated an hour and a half before dinner. I am not sure whether I have mentioned that, when Mr Micawber was at any particularly desperate crisis, he used a sort of legal phraseology: which he seemed to think equivalent to winding up his affairs.

This was the letter.

"Sir—for I dare not say my dear Copperfield,

"It is expedient that I should inform you that the undersigned is Crushed. Some flickering efforts to spare you the premature knowledge of his calamitous position, you may observe in him this day; but hope has sunk beneath the horizon, and the undersigned is Crushed.

"The present communication is penned within the personal range (I cannot call it the society) of an individual, in a state closely bordering on intoxication, employed by a broker. That individual is in legal possession of the premises, under a distress for rent. His inventory includes, not only the chattels and effects of every description belonging to the undersigned, as yearly tenant of this habitation, but also those appertaining to Mr. Thomas Traddles, lodger, a member of the Honourable Society of the Inner Temple.

"If any drop of gloom were wanting in the overflowing cup, which is now 'commended' (in the language of an immortal Writer) to the lips of the undersigned, it would be found in the fact, that a friendly acceptance granted to the undersigned, by the before-mentioned Mr. Thomas Traddles, for the sum of £23 4*s* 9½*d* is over due and is NOT provided for. Also, in the fact, that the living responsibilities clinging to the undersigned, will, in the course of nature be increased by the sum of one more helpless victim; whose miserable appearance may be looked for—in round numbers—at the expiration of a period not exceeding six lunar months from the present date.

"After premising thus much, it would be a work of supererogation to add, that dust and ashes are for ever scattered

"On

"The

"Head

"Of

"WILKINS MICAWBER"

CHAPTER IV.

Seldom did I wake at night, seldom did I look up at the moon or stars or watch the falling rain, or hear the wind, but I thought of the solitary figure of the good fisherman toiling on—poor Pilgrim!—and recalled his words, "I'm a going to seek my niece. I'm a going to seek her fur and wide."

Months passed, and he had been absent—no one knew where—the whole time.

It had been a bitter day in London, and a cutting north-east wind had blown. The wind had gone down with the light, and snow had come on.

My shortest way home,—and I naturally took the shortest way on such a night—was through Saint Martin's Lane. On the steps of the church, there was the figure of a man. And I stood face to face with Mr. Peggotty!

"Mas'r Davy! It do my art good to see you, sir. Well met, well met!"

"Well met, my dear old friend!"

"I had thowts o' coming to make inquiration for you, sir, to-night, but it was too late. I should have come early in the morning, sir, afore going away agen."

"Again?"

"Yes, sir, I'm away to-morrow."

In those days there was a side entrance to the stable-yard of the Golden

Cross Inn. Two or three public-rooms opened out of the yard; and looking into one of them, and finding it empty, and a good fire burning, I took him in there.

"I'll tell you, Mas'r Davy, wheer all I've been, and what-all we've heerd. I've been fur, and we've heerd little; but I'll tell you!"

As he sat thinking, there was a fine massive gravity in his face, which I did not venture to disturb.

"You see, Sir—, When she was a child, she used to talk to me a deal about the sea, and about them coasts where the sea got to be dark blue, and to lay a shining and a shining in the sun.

"When she was—lost, I know'd in my mind, as he would take her to them countries. I know'd in my mind, as he'd have told her wonders of 'em, and how she was to be a lady theer, and how he first got her to listen to him along o' sech like. I went across-channel to France, and landed theer, as if I'd fell down from the skies. I found out a English gentleman, as was in authority, and told him I was going to seek my niece. He got me them papers as I wanted fur to carry me through—I doen't rightly know how they're called—and he would have give me money, but that I was thankful to have no need on. I thank him kind, for all he done, I'm sure! I told him, best as I was able, what my gratitoode was, and went away through France, fur to seek my niece."

"Alone, and on foot?"

"Mostly a-foot; sometimes in carts along with people going to market; sometimes in empty coaches. Many mile a day a-foot, and often with some poor soldier or another, travelling fur to see his friends. I couldn't talk to him, nor he to me; but we was company for one another, too, along the dusty roads. When I come to any town, I found the inn, and waited about the yard till some one came by (some one mostly did) as know'd English. Then I told how that I was on my way to seek my niece, and they told me what manner of gentlefolks was in the house, and I waited to see any as seemed like her, going in or out. When it warn't Em'ly, I went on agen. By little and little, when I come to a new village or that, among the poor people, I found they know'd about me. They would set me down at their cottage doors, and give me what-not fur to eat and drink, and show me where to sleep. And many a woman, Mas'r Davy, as has had a daughter of about Em'ly's age, I've found a-waiting for me, at Our Saviour's Cross outside the village, fur to do me sim'lar kindnesses. Some has had daughters as was dead. And God only knows how good them mothers was to me!"

I laid my trembling hand upon the hand he put before his face. "Thankee, sir, doen't take no notice."

"At last I come to the sea. It warn't hard, you may suppose, for a seafaring man like me to work his way over to Italy. When I got theer, I wandered on as I had done afore. I got news of her being seen among them Swiss mountains yonder. I made for them mountains, day and night. Ever so fur as I went, ever so fur them mountains seemed to shift away from me. But I come up with 'em, and I crossed 'em. I never doubted her. No! Not a bit! On'y let her see my face—on'y let her heer my voice—on'y let my stanning still afore her bring to her thoughts the home she had fled away from, and the child she had been—and if she had growed to be a royal lady, she'd have fell down at my feet! I know'd it well! I bought a country dress to put upon her. To put that dress upon her, and to cast off what she wore—to take her on my arm again, and wander towards home—to stop sometimes upon the road, and heal her bruised feet and her worse-bruised heart—was all I thowt of now. But, Mas'r Davy, it warn't to be—not yet! I was too late, and they was gone. Wheer, I couldn't learn. Some said heer, some said theer. I travelled heer, and I travelled theer, but I found no Em'ly, and I travelled home."

"How long ago?"

"A matter o' fewer days. I sighted the old boat arter dark, and I never could have thowt, I'm sure, that the old boat would have been so strange!"

From some pocket in his breast, he took out with a very careful hand, a small paper bundle containing two or three letters or little packets, which he laid upon the table.

"The faithful creetur Mrs Gummidge gave me these. This first one come afore I had been gone a week. A fifty pound Bank note, in a sheet of paper, directed to me, and put underneath the door in the night. She tried to hide her writing, but she couldn't hide it from Me! This one come to Missis Gummidge, two or three months ago. Five pounds."

It was untouched like the previous sum, and he refolded both.

"Is that another letter in your hand?"

"It's money too, sir. Ten pound, you see. And wrote inside, 'From a true friend.' But the two first was put underneath the door, and this come by the post, day afore yesterday. I'm going to seek her at the post-mark."

He showed it to me. It was a town on the Upper Rhine. He had found out, at Yarmouth, some foreign dealers who knew that country, and they had drawn him a rude map on paper, which he could very well understand.

I asked him how Ham was?

"He works as bold as a man can. He's never been heerd fur to complain. But my belief is ('twixt ourselves) as it has cut him deep. Well! Having seen you to-night, Mas'r Davy (and that doos me good!), I shall away betimes to-morrow morning. You have seen what I've got heer;" putting his hand on where the little packet lay; "all that troubles me is, to think that any harm might come to me, afore this money was give back. If I was to die, and it was lost, or stole, or elseways made away with, and it was never know'd by him but what I'd accepted of it, I believe the t'other wureld wouldn't hold me! I believe I must come back!"

He rose, and I rose too. We grasped each other by the hand again, and as we went out into the rigorous night, everything seemed to be hushed in reverence for him, when he resumed his solitary journey through the snow.

CHAPTER V

ALL this time I had gone on loving Dora harder than ever. If I may so express it, I was steeped in Dora. I was not merely over head and ears in love with her; I was saturated through and through. I took night walks to Norwood where she lived, and perambulated round and round the house and garden for hours together; looking through crevices in the palings, using violent exertions to get my chin above the rusty nails on the top, blowing kisses at the lights in the windows, and romantically calling on the night to shield my Dora. I don't exactly know from what—I suppose from fire—perhaps from mice, to which she had a great objection.

Dora had a discreet friend, comparatively stricken in years—almost of the ripe age of twenty, I should say—whose name was Miss Mills. Dora called her Julia. She was the bosom friend of Dora. Happy Miss Mills!

One day Miss Mills said, "Dora is coming to stay with me. She is coming the day after to-morrow. If you would like to call, I am sure papa would be happy to see you."

I passed three days in a luxury of wretchedness, and at last, arrayed for the purpose at a vast expense, I went to Miss Mills's fraught with a declaration.

Mr. Mills was not at home. I didn't expect he would be. Nobody wanted *him.* Miss Mills was at home. Miss Mills would do.

I was shown into a room up-stairs, where Miss Mills and Dora were. Dora's little dog Jip was there. Miss Mills was copying music, and Dora was painting flowers. What were my feelings when I recognized flowers I had given her!

Miss Mills was very glad to see me, and very sorry her papa was not at home: though I thought we all bore that with fortitude. Miss Mills was conversational for a few minutes, and then, laying down her pen, got up and left the room.

I began to think I would put it off till to-morrow.

"I hope your poor horse was not tired, when he got home at night from that pic-nic," said Dora, lifting up her beautiful eyes. "It was a long way for him."

I began to think I would do it to-day.

"It was a long way for *him*, for *he* had nothing to uphold him on the journey."

"Wasn't he fed, poor thing?" asked Dora.

I began to think I would put it off till to-morrow.

"Ye—yes, he was well taken care of. I mean he had not the unutterable happiness that I had in being so near you."

I saw now that I was in for it, and it must be done on the spot.

"I don't know why you should care for being near me," said Dora, "or why you should call it a happiness. But of course you don't mean what you say. Jip, you naughty boy, come here!"

I don't know how I did it, but I did it in a moment. I intercepted Jip. I had Dora in my arms. I was full of eloquence. I never stopped for a word. I told her how I loved her. I told her I should die without her. I told her that I idolized and worshipped her. Jip barked madly all the time.

My eloquence increased and I said, if she would like me to die for her, she had but to say the word, and I was ready. I had loved her to distraction every minute, day and night, since I first set eyes upon her. I loved her at that minute to distraction. I should always love her, every minute, to distraction. Lovers had loved before, and lovers would love again; but no lover had ever loved, might, could, would, or should, ever love, as I loved Dora. The more I raved, the more Jip barked. Each of us, in his own way, got more mad every moment.

Well, well! Dora and I were sitting on the sofa by-and-by, quiet enough, and Jip was lying in her lap, winking peacefully at me. It was off my mind. I was in a state of perfect rapture. Dora and I were engaged.

Being poor, I felt it necessary the next time I went to my darling, to expatiate on that unfortunate drawback. I soon carried desolation into the bosom of our joys—not that I meant to do it, but that I was so full of the subject—by asking Dora, without the smallest preparation, if she could love a beggar?

Sprightly laugh

"How can you ask me anything so foolish? Love a beggar!"

"Dora, my own dearest! *I* am a beggar!"

"How can you be such a silly thing," replied Dora, slapping my hand, "as to sit there, telling such stories? I'll make Jip bite you if you are so ridiculous."

But I looked so serious, that Dora began to cry. She did nothing but exclaim Oh dear! Oh dear! And oh, she was so frightened! And where was Julia Mills! And oh, take her to Julia Mills, and go away, please! until I was almost beside myself.

I thought I had killed her. I sprinkled water on her face. I went down on my knees. I plucked at my hair. I implored her forgiveness. I besought her to look up. I ravaged Miss Mills's work-box for a smelling-bottle, and in my agony of mind applied an ivory needle-case instead, and dropped all the needles over Dora.

At last, I got Dora to look at me, with a horrified expression which I gradually soothed until it was only loving, and her soft, pretty cheek was lying against mine.

"Is your heart mine still, dear Dora?"

"Oh, yes! Oh, yes, it's all yours. Oh, don't be dreadful!"

I dreadful. To Dora!

"Don't talk about being poor, and working hard! Oh, don't, don't!"

"My dearest love, the crust well earned—"

"Oh, yes; but I don't want to hear any more about crusts! And after we are married, Jip must have a mutton-chop every day at twelve, or he'll die!"

I was charmed with her childish, winning way, and I fondly explained to

her that Jip should have his mutton-chop with his accustomed regularity.

When we had been engaged some half a year or so, Dora delighted me by asking me to give her that cookery-book I had once spoken of, and to show her how to keep housekeeping accounts, as I had once promised I would. I brought the volume with me on my next visit (I got it prettily bound, first, to make it look less dry and more inviting); and showed her an old house-keeping-book of my aunt's, and gave her a set of tablets, and a pretty little pencil-case, and a box of leads, to practise house-keeping with.

But the cookery-book made Dora's head ache, and the figures made her cry. They wouldn't add up, she said. So she rubbed them out, and drew little nosegays, and likenesses of me and Jip, all over the tablets.

Time went on, and at last, here in this hand of mine I held the wedding licence. There were the two names in the sweet old visionary connexion, David Copperfield and Dora Spenlow; and there in the corner was that parental Institution the Stamp-office, looking down upon our union; and there, in the printed form of words, was the Archbishop of Canterbury invoking a blessing on us, and doing it as cheap as could possibly be expected!

I doubt whether two young birds could have known less about keeping house, than I and my pretty Dora did. We had a servant, of course. She kept house for us. We had an awful time of it with Mary Anne.

Her name was Paragon. Her nature was represented to us, when we engaged her, as being feebly expressed in her name. She had a written character, as large as a Proclamation; and, according to this document, could do everything of a domestic nature that ever I heard of, and a great many things that I never did hear of. She was a woman in the prime of life; of a severe countenance; and subject (particularly in the arms) to a sort of perpetual measles. She had a cousin in the Life Guards, with such long legs that he looked like the afternoon shadow of somebody else. She was warranted sober and honest. And I am therefore willing to believe that she was in a fit when we found her under the boiler; and that the deficient teaspoons were attributable to the dustman. She was the cause of our first little quarrel.

"My dearest life," I said one day to Dora, "do you think Mary Anne has any idea of time?"

"Why, Doady?"

"My love, because it's five, and we were to have dined at four."

My little wife came and sat upon my knee, to coax me to be quiet, and drew a line with her pencil down the middle of my nose; but I couldn't dine off that, though it was very agreeable.

"Don't you think, my dear, it would be better for you to remonstrate with Mary Anne?"

"Oh no, please! I couldn't, Doady!"

"Why not, my love?"

"Oh, because I am such a little goose, and she knows I am!"

I thought this sentiment so incompatible with the establishment of any system of check on Mary Anne, that I frowned a little.

"My precious wife, we must be serious sometimes. Come! Sit down on this chair, close beside me! Give me the pencil! There! Now let us talk sensibly. You know, dear;" what a little hand it was to hold, and what a tiny wedding-ring it was to see! "You know, my love, it is not exactly comfortable to have to go out without one's dinner. Now, is it?"

"N—n—no!" replied Dora, faintly.

"My love, how you tremble!"

"Because I KNOW you're going to scold me."

"My sweet, I am only going to reason."

"Oh, but reasoning is worse than scolding! I didn't marry to be reasoned with. If you meant to reason with such a poor little thing as I am, you ought to have told me so, you cruel boy!"

"Now, my own Dora, you are childish, and are talking nonsense. You must remember, I am sure, that I was obliged to go out yesterday when dinner was half over; and that, the day before, I was made quite unwell by being obliged to eat underdone veal in a hurry; to-day, I don't dine at all—and I am afraid to say how long we waited for breakfast—and *then* the water didn't boil. I don't mean to reproach you, my dear, but this is not comfortable."

"I wonder, I do, at your making such ungrateful speeches. When you know that the other day, when you said you would like a little bit of fish, I went out myself, miles and miles, and ordered it, to surprise you."

"And it was very kind of you, my own darling, and I felt it so much that I wouldn't on any account have mentioned that you bought a salmon—which was too much for two. Or that it cost one pound six—which was more than we can afford."

"You enjoyed it very much," sobbed Dora. "And you said I was a mouse."

"And I'll say so again, my love, a thousand times!"

I said it a thousand times, and more, and went on saying it until Mary Anne's cousin deserted into our coal-hole, and was brought out, to our great amazement, by a piquet of his companions in arms, who took him away handcuffed, in a procession that covered our front-garden with disgrace.

Everybody we had anything to do with, seemed to cheat us. Our appearance in a shop was a signal for the damaged goods to be brought out immediately. If we bought a lobster, it was full of water. All our meat turned out tough, and there was hardly any crust to our loaves.

As to the washerwoman pawning the clothes, and coming in a state of penitent intoxication to apologize, I suppose that might have happened several times to anybody. Also the chimney on fire, the parish engine, and perjury on the part of the Beadle. But I apprehend we were personally unfortunate in our page: whose principal function was to quarrel with the cook. He lived in a hail of saucepan-lids. We wanted to get rid of him, but he was very much attached to us, and wouldn't go, until one day he stole Dora's watch, and spent the produce (he was always a weak-minded boy) in riding up and down between London and Uxbridge outside the coach. He was taken to the Police Office, on the completion of his fifteenth journey; when four-and-sixpence, and a second-hand fife which he couldn't play, were found upon his person.

He was tried and ordered to be transported. Even then he couldn't be quiet, but was always writing us letters; and he wanted so much to see Dora before he went away, that Dora went to visit him, and fainted when she found herself inside the iron bars. I had no peace of my life until he was expatriated, and made (as I afterwards heard) a shepherd of, "up the country" somewhere; I have no geographical idea where.

"I am very sorry for all this, Doady," said Dora. "Will you call me a name I want you to call me?"

"What is it, my dear?"

"It's a stupid name—Child-wife. When you are going to be angry with me, say to yourself 'it's only my Child-wife.' When I am very disappointing, say, 'I knew, a long time ago, that she would make but a Child-wife.' When you miss what you would like me to be, and what I should like to be, and what I think I never can be, say, 'Still my foolish Child-wife loves me.' For indeed I do."

I invoke the innocent figure that I dearly loved, to come out of the mists and shadows of the Past, and to turn its gentle head towards me once again, and to bear witness that it was made happy by what I answered.

CHAPTER VI

I HEARD a footstep on the stairs one day. I knew it to be Mr. Peggotty's. It came nearer, nearer rushed into the room.

"Mas'r Davy, I've found her! I thank my Heavenly Father for having guided of me in His own ways to my darling!"

"And may my prayers go up to Heaven that 'twill be a happiness to her, and a comfort, and a honour, all her life! May it love her and be dootiful to her in her old age; helpful of her at the last; a Angel to her heer, and heerafter! Em'ly told her, and she took her to her home. Theer, Em'ly was took bad with fever, and fell into the weakness of the littlest child.

"When she got strong again, she cast about. She got to France, and took service to wait on travelling ladies at a inn in the port. Theer, theer come, one day that snake. —Let him never come nigh me. —Soon as she see him, without him seeing her, she fled afore the very breath he draw'd. She come to England, and was set ashore at Dover. All the way to England she had thowt to come right straight to her dear home. But fear of not being forgiv, fear of being pinted at, fear of some of us being dead along of her, fear of many things, turned her from it, kiender by force, upon the road.

"She come to London. She—as had never seen it in her life—alone—without a penny—young—so pretty—come to London.

"Mas'r Davy! I know'd of bitter knowledge wheer to watch and what to do. And the Lord was above all! I come upon her in her sleep. She woke, caught sight of me, and swouned away. I wrapped her, hasty, in her clothes. I took her in my arms. I kissed her face. I laid it heer, and hid it with a hankecher. I brought her safe out, last night as her was. All night long, her arms has been about my neck, and her head has laid heer; and we knows full well, as we can put our trust in one another evermore."

He ceased to speak, and his hand upon the table rested there in perfect repose, with a resolution in it that might have conquered lions.

"You have made up your mind as to the future, good friend?"

"Yes, Mas'r Davy, theer's mighty countries, fur from heer. Our future life lays over the sea."

As he gave me both his hands, hurrying to return to the one charge of his noble existence, I thought of Ham and who would break the intelligence to him? Mr. Peggotty thought of everything. He had already written to the poor fellow, and had the letter in the pocket of his rough coat, ready for the post. I asked him for it, and said I would go down to Yarmouth, and talk to Ham myself before I gave it him, and prepare him for its contents. He thanked me very earnestly, and we parted, with the understanding that I would go down by the Mail that same night. In the evening I started.

"Don't you think that," I asked the coachman, in the first stage out of London, "a very remarkable sky? I don't remember to have ever seen one like it."

"Nor I. That's wind, sir. There'll be mischief done at sea before long."

It was a murky confusion of flying clouds tossed up into most remarkable heaps, through which the wild moon seemed to plunge headlong, as if, in a dread disturbance of the laws of nature, she had lost her way. There had been a wind all day; and it was rising then, with an extraordinary great sound. In another hour it had much increased, and the sky was more overcast, and it blew hard.

But, as the night advanced, the wind blew harder and harder. I had been in Yarmouth when the seamen said it blew great guns, but I had never known the like of this, or anything approaching to it.

The tremendous sea itself, when I came to my journey's end, confounded me. As the high watery walls came rolling in, and tumbled into surf, I seemed to see a rending and upheaving of all nature.

Not finding Ham among the people whom this memorable wind had brought together on the beach, I made my way to his house. I learned that he had gone, on a job of shipwright's work, some miles away, but that he would be back to-morrow morning, in good time.

So, I went back to the inn; and when I had washed and dressed, and tried to sleep, but in vain, it was late in the afternoon. I had not sat five minutes by the coffee-room fire, when the waiter coming to stir it, told me that two

colliers had gone down, with all hands, a few miles off; and that some other ships had been seen labouring hard in the Roads, and trying, in great distress, to keep off shore. Mercy on them, and on all poor sailors, said he, if we had another night like the last!

I could not eat, I could not sit still, I could not continue stedfast to anything. My dinner went away almost untasted, and I tried to refresh myself with a glass or two of wine. In vain. I walked to and fro, tried to read an old gazetteer, listened to the awful noises: looked at faces, scenes, and figures in the fire. At length the ticking of the undisturbed clock on the wall, tormented me to that degree that I resolved to go to bed.

For hours I lay in bed listening to the wind and water; imagining, now, that I heard shrieks out at sea; now, that I distinctly heard the firing of signal guns; now, the fall of houses in the town. At length, my restlessness attained to such a pitch, that I hurried on my clothes, and went down-stairs. In the large kitchen, all the inn servants and some other watchers were clustered together. One man asked me when I went in among them whether I thought the souls of the collier-crews who had gone down, were out in the storm?

There was a dark gloom in my lonely chamber, when I at length returned to it; but I was tired now, and getting into bed again, fell into the depths of sleep until broad day when I was aroused, at eight or nine o'clock, by some one knocking and calling at my door.

"What is the matter?"

"A wreck! Close by!"

"What wreck?"

"A schooner, from Spain or Portugal, laden with fruit and wine. Make haste, sir, if you want to see her! It's thought, down on the beach, she'll go to pieces every moment."

Quick

I wrapped myself in my clothes as quickly as I could, and ran into the street, where numbers of people were before me, all running in one direction—to the beach.

When I got there,— in the difficulty of hearing anything but wind and waves, and in the crowd, and the unspeakable confusion, and my first breathless

efforts to stand against the weather, I was so confused that I looked out to sea for the wreck, and saw nothing but the foaming heads of the great waves. A boatman laid a hand upon my arm, and pointed. Then, I saw it, close in upon us!

One mast was broken short off, six or eight feet from the deck, and lay over the side, entangled in a maze of sail and rigging; and all that ruin, as the ship rolled and beat—which she did with a violence quite inconceivable—beat the side as if it would stave it in. Some efforts were being made, to cut this portion of the wreck away; for, as the ship, which was broadside on, turned towards us in her rolling, I plainly descried her people at work with axes—especially one active figure with long curling hair. But a great cry, audible even above the wind and water, rose from the shore; the sea, sweeping over the wreck, made a clean breach, and carried men, spars, casks, planks, bulwarks, heaps of such toys, into the boiling surge.

The second mast was yet standing, with the rags of a sail, and a wild confusion of broken cordage flapping to and fro. The ship had struck once, the same boatman said, and then lifted in and struck again. I understood him to add that she was parting amidships. As he spoke, there was another great cry of pity from the beach. Four men arose with the wreck out of the deep, clinging to the rigging of the remaining mast; uppermost, the active figure with the curling hair.

There was a bell on board; and as the ship rolled and dashed, this bell rang; and its sound, the knell of those unhappy men, was borne towards us on the wind. Again we lost her, and again she rose. Two of the four men were gone. I noticed that some new sensation moved the people on the beach, and saw them part, and Ham come breaking through them to the front.

Instantly, I ran to him, for I divined that he meant to wade off with an axe rope. I held him back with both arms; and implored the men not to listen to him, not to let him stir that sand!

Another cry arose; and we saw the cruel sail, with blow on blow, beat off the lower of the two men, and fly up in triumph round the active figure left alone upon the mast.

Against such a sight, and against such determination as that of the calmly desperate man who was already accustomed to lead half the people present, I might as hopefully have entreated the wind.

I was swept away to some distance, where the people around me made me stay; urging, as I confusedly perceived, that he was bent on going, with help or without, and that I should endanger the precautions for his safety by troubling those with whom they rested. I saw hurry on the beach, and men running with ropes and penetrating into a circle of figures that hid him from me. —Then, I saw him standing alone, in a seaman's frock and trowsers: a rope in his hand: another round his body: and several of the best men holding to the latter.

The wreck was breaking up. I saw that she was parting in the middle, and that the life of the solitary man upon the mast hung by a thread. He had a singular red cap on, —not like a sailor's cap, but of a finer colour; and as the few planks between him and destruction rolled and bulged, and as his death-knell rung, he was seen by all of us to wave his cap. I saw him do it now, and thought I was going distracted, when his action brought an old remembrance to my mind of a once dear friend—*the* once dear friend—Steerforth.

Ham watched the sea, until there was a great retiring wave; when he dashed in after it, and in a moment was buffeting with the water, rising with the hills, falling with the valleys, lost beneath the foam; borne in towards the shore, borne on towards the ship. At length he neared the wreck. He was so near, that with one more of his vigorous strokes he would be clinging to it,—when, a high green vast hill-side of water, moving on shoreward, from beyond the ship, he seemed to leap up into it with a mighty bound—and the ship was gone!

Low

They drew him to my very feet—insensible—dead. He was carried to the nearest house; and every means of restoration were tried; but he had been beaten to death by the great wave, and his generous heart was stilled for ever.

Lower

As I sat beside the bed, when hope was abandoned and all was done, a fisherman, who had known me when Emily and I were children, and ever since, whispered my name at the door.

"Sir, will you come over yonder?"

The old remembrance that had been recalled to me, was in his look. I asked him:

"Has a body come ashore?"

"Yes."

"Do I know it?"

He answered nothing. But, he led me to the shore. And on that part of it where she and I had looked for shells, two children—on that part of it where some lighter fragments of the old boat, blown down last night, had been scattered by the wind—among the ruins of the home he had wronged—I saw him lying with his head upon his arm, as I had often seen him lie at school.

THE END OF THE READING

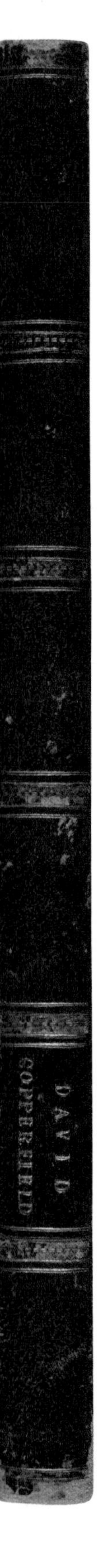

Dickens and the Berg Collection of The New York Public Library

A WORLD-CLASS collection of Charles Dickens's books and papers has long been a renowned adornment of The New York Public Library's Henry W. and Albert A. Berg Collection of English and American Literature. One of America's most celebrated assemblages of literary first editions, rare books, autograph letters, and manuscripts, the Berg includes some 35,000 printed items and 2,000 linear feet of manuscripts and archives of more than four hundred authors.

The founding collection was presented to the Library in 1940, with an endowment, by Dr. Albert A. Berg in memory of his late brother, Dr. Henry W. Berg. By the time of Henry's death in 1938, the Drs. Berg had assembled a distinguished library consisting of approximately 3,500 volumes, focusing primarily on important first editions and other rare books by more than one hundred British and American authors. Dickens accounted for a tenth of the holdings.

The Berg's extensive collection of Dickens imprints and papers has grown to include, for six of his novels, the serialized "in-parts" editions in which they were first issued; prompt copies for twelve of his works; the first separate editions of all of his novels; copies inscribed by Dickens to notables and friends; all of his periodical contributions; suites of drawings by Dickens's illustrators; manuscripts of a few occasional writings; the 1867-68 date book of his second tour of America; more than five hundred letters in his hand; and numerous objects owned by him.

Dickens's personal prompt copy of *David Copperfield,* from which this facsimile was made, is one of the great treasures of the Berg Collection. Heavily marked up by Dickens with annotations, cuts, revisions, and stage directions to himself, this prompt copy is a one-of-a-kind record of how he perfected the text for his public performances. The original was bound up for Dickens, with his bookplate, and added to his library at Gad's Hill Place.

The spine of Dickens's prompt copy of *David Copperfield*

Acknowledgments

OUR THANKS to Dr. Anthony W. Marx, President and CEO of The New York Public Library, for encouraging this partnership between the Library and Levenger, and to Mark Charles Dickens, for graciously granting the Library permission to publish his great-great-grandfather's prompt copy.

We are ever grateful to Sara Abraham, the Library's steadfast champion of this project, and are once again in awe of Isaac Gewirtz's talent for telling the Dickens story like no other. Kenneth Benson provided answers and guidance for every question (including those we didn't know to ask) with his customary enthusiasm and generosity. Terrance D'Ambrosio and Pete Riesett braved weather most foul to deliver the images of this Library treasure for the making of the facsimile, and we thank them.

Uncommon Books for Thoughtful Readers

A Christmas Carol: The Original 1843 Manuscript
Charles Dickens

Christopher Columbus Book of Privileges
Daniel De Simone, John W. Hessler and Chet Van Duzer

The *Fantasia* of Leonardo da Vinci
Ross King

The Grimani Breviary
Foreword by Ross King

John F. Kennedy: The Making of His Inaugural Address
Commentary by Roger G. Kennedy

Long Remembered: Lincoln and His Five Versions of the Gettysburg Address
Douglas L. Wilson et al.

The Making of The Finest Hour
Speech by Winston S. Churchill
Introduction by Richard M. Langworth

Notes on Our Times
E. B. White

On Contentedness of Mind
Plutarch
Introduced by Ralph Waldo Emerson

On a Life Well Spent
Cicero
Preface by Benjamin Franklin

Painting as a Pastime
Winston S. Churchill

The Prompt Copy of *A Christmas Carol*
Charles Dickens

Redouté: The Grand Collection
A portfolio of botanical masterpieces

The Sarajevo Haggadah
Authorized facsimile of the 14th-century original

Seeing the World Anew: The Radical Vision of Martin Waldseemüller's 1507 & 1516 World Maps
John W. Hessler and Chet Van Duzer

The Silverado Squatters
Robert Louis Stevenson

The Starry Messenger
Galileo Galilei
John W. Hessler and Daniel De Simone, eds.

Thoreau on Cape Cod: His Journeys and the Lost Maps
Henry David Thoreau
Commentary by John Hessler

Thoreau's Maine Woods: A Photographic Journey
Scot Miller

"What I began by reading, I must finish by acting."
Henry David Thoreau